MERCILESS
Saints

USA TODAY BESTSELLING AUTHOR
MICHELLE HEARD

Copyright © 2021 by M.A. Heard.

All rights reserved. No part of this publication may be reproduced, distributed, or transmitted in any form or by any means, including photocopying, recording, or other electronic or mechanical methods, without the prior written consent of the publisher, except in the case of brief quotation embodied in critical reviews and various other noncommercial uses permitted by copyright law.

The resemblance to actual persons, things, living or dead, locales, or events is entirely coincidental.

Cover Designer: Cormar Covers

TABLE OF CONTENTS

Dedication

Songlist

Synopsis

Merciless Saints

Family Tree

Chapter 1

Chapter 2

Chapter 3

Chapter 4

Chapter 5

Chapter 6

Chapter 7

Chapter 8

Chapter 9

Chapter 10

Chapter 11

Chapter 12

Chapter 13

Chapter 14

Chapter 15

Chapter 16

Chapter 17

Chapter 18

Chapter 19

Chapter 20

Chapter 21

Chapter 22

Chapter 23

Chapter 24

Chapter 25

Chapter 26

Chapter 27

Epilogue

Published Books

Connect with me

About the author

Acknowledgments

Dedication

To Clarissa.
Thank you for mentoring me.
You've been priceless in my journey as an author.
I hope to see you in person soon.

———————

Songlist

Never Surrender – Liv Ash

Devil Devil – MILCK

The Wolf In Your Darkest Room – Matthew Mayfield

Nothing Is As It Seems – Hidden Citizens, Ruelle

Far From Home – Sam Tinnesz

The Devil Within – Matthew Mayfield

Dark Matter – Les Friction

Caught In The Fire – Klergy

We All Bleed – Roenin

Dark Side – Cece And The Dark Hearts

Living In The Shadows – Matthew Perryman Jones

If I Burn – Tara Lee

Real World – Ryan Star

The Parting Glass – The Wailin' Jennys

In The Air Tonight – Joseph Willian Morgan

Don't Fear The Reaper – The Spiritual Machines

When The Darkness Comes – Colbie Caillat

Follow You Down – Matthew Mayfield

My Love Will Never Die – AG, Claire Wyndham

Why We Try – Matthew Mayfield, Chelsea Lankes

Synopsis

Alliances are made. Loyalty is owned. Love is taken.

I'll show everyone I'm a threat, and they will fear me.
For my family. I have to protect them.

The second I hear the name Damien Vetrov I know I'm in trouble.
He's an arrogant Russian God.
Only, I have zero intention of bowing to him. Ever.
Attractive and lethal. He's such an intoxicating mixture.

Every second we spend together, the pull between us becomes stronger, and my fear grows.
While my body wants him, my head knows better. He has the power to kill my family.

But when blood is shed, I'm forced to depend on Damien for my life.

Being at his mercy, whether he'll kill me or protect me, is still up for debate.

Merciless Saints

Mafia / Organized Crime / Suspense Romance
COMPLETE STANDALONES.

Family Tree

Damien Vetrov
↓
Demitri Vetrov
Brother

Family Business: Custodians.

Father: Deceased

Uncle: Michail Vetrov

Winter Hemsley
↓
Patrick 'Pat' Hemsley
Father

Nicknames: Blood Princess

Personal Guard: Cillian Byrne

Brother: Sean Hemsley

Mother: Deceased

Family Business: Blood Diamond dealers.

Chapter 1

WINTER

The Past - 13 Years Old.

"Winter," Mom calls from the other side of the store, "what do you think of this one?"

Dropping the beanie I was looking at, I walk closer to Mom and stare at the jacket she's holding up. "It's pink."

Her lips curve into a warm smile. "You love pink."

"Not anymore." I move past her to the rack of jackets and glance over the selection until I find a black one. "I like this one more."

Mom's eyes widen slightly. "Please tell me you're not going to start wearing only black now that you're a teenager."

I shrug as I remove the jacket from the rack. "Pink is too girlie. Black will tell the other kids not to mess with me."

Mom lets out a chuckle while shaking her head lightly. "Black it is then."

We spend the next hour shopping for my winter wardrobe. I only choose blacks, grays, and whites, avoiding any other color, which Mom's not too happy about.

Tomorrow I'll leave for private school, and I want everything to be perfect. I might only be thirteen, but even I know first impressions count a lot. Being smaller than most girls my age makes me an easy target for bullies, so I have to do everything I can to show the other girls attending the school I'm not to be messed with.

While one of our guards takes the bags to the car, Mom wraps an arm around my shoulders. "Do you want to stop for lunch or head home?"

Thinking of my father and brother, I reply, "We can get pizza to take home so Daddy and Sean can have some as well."

"Good idea," Mom agrees, steering me toward a Pizza Hut.

Mom chooses a vegetable supreme, while I select a Hawaiian for myself and a mega meaty for Dad and Sean.

Once our order is ready, one of the guards, Patrick, carries the boxes. As we leave the mall, I think about all the packing I have to do. Pushing my luck, I glance up at Mom and ask, "Will you help me pack?"

Mom grins down at me. "Of course."

Walking toward the car, our guards fan out around us. It's something I've gotten so used to. I hardly notice them.

"Down!" I hear Cillian shout, but before we're able to move, gunfire erupts around us.

Patrick drops the pizza to the ground and yanks his gun out. He reaches for Mom's arm, and as he begins to move in front of her, bullets spray over us. Three hit Patrick, and my eyes widen as my mouth drops open in a scream.

A piercing pain slices through my neck, and I hear Mom wail as she throws her body toward mine. Mom grabs hold of me and yanks me down to the ground.

My eyes dart in the direction the gunfire is coming from, and I watch as Cillian takes down the men shooting at us until they're all dead. The sight should horrify me, but I'm too shocked to react.

Cillian runs toward me, and dropping down to his knees, he breathes, "Winter… Rose?"

Only then do I glance down to where Mom's head is resting on my chest. Blood spirals across her forehead from a hole just beneath her hairline.

"Mom," I groan. A merciless ache blossoms in my chest, and it threatens to strip me of my sanity. Even though I know she's dead, I still struggle out from under her, and grabbing hold of her shoulders, I begin to shake her. "Mommy!" Panicked breaths explode over my lips as my body jerks. "Mommy!" I cry, devastating hopelessness seeping into my bones. I begin to scream as hysteria engulfs me.

She can't be dead. Not my mom.

No.

Gasping for air, I can't think clearly anymore.

Cillian grabs hold of my arm, trying to pull me away from Mom.

"No!" I scream at him, trying to worm myself free from his hold so I can stay with Mom.

"We have to go, poppet. It's not safe," he snaps at me.

"No!" I scream again, refusing to leave Mom. I grip hold of her white shirt, curling my fingers into the fabric as my gaze locks on the blood staining her pale skin.

This isn't real.

Then it sinks in like a lump of burning coal.

Mom's dead.

Cries begin to tear through me as I drop my forehead to Mom's chest. Sobs wrack through me as my tears fall to her shirt.

Minutes ago, I was Rose Hemsleys precious little girl.

Minutes ago, she was smiling at me.

Minutes ago, I had a mom who loved me more than anything.

"Holy mother of saints," Cillian suddenly hisses, and then he grabs hold of me. I'm yanked into the air as he climbs to his feet, and holding me tightly, he runs toward the car. My cries turn to whimpers as unbearable heartache swamps me.

I watch as the distance between Mom and me keeps growing. A breeze picks up, making some of her ginger hair blow over her face, sticking to the blood.

'Mommy,' my heart wails. My innocence is ripped from me, and my world is thrown into violent disarray.

Cillian bundles me into the passenger seat and straps on the seat belt before he slams the door shut. I watch him run around the front of the car. He climbs behind the steering wheel, and seconds later, tires squeal as we race away from the gruesome sight.

"We can't leave Mom," I cry.

Something slams into the car, and we jerk forward. My cries grow louder when Cillian curses, his hands tightening on the steering wheel.

Bullets hit my side of the car, and terrified, I scream.

"Get down, Winter!" Cillian shouts at me.

With trembling fingers, I unbuckle the seat belt and slip off the seat. More bullets hit the car, and the windows shatter, raining glass down on me.

"Fucking bastards," Cillian growls as he does his best to keep the car on the road. Something slams into us again, making the vehicle jerk forward.

"Almost there," Cillian grinds the words out as he takes a sharp corner, making the tires screech as they struggle to stay on the road.

I glance up at Cillian, and the worry etched with deep lines on his face makes grave fear shudder through me. I've never seen Cillian scared before. He's always been calm. He always looked at me with a lopsided grin. Being my personal guard Cillian was always just there, walking a couple of steps ahead of me. Now he's the only thing standing between me and the monsters who killed my mom.

Another wave of bullets sprays the car. Cillian lets out a string of curses as he pushes his foot down on the peddle.

"Stay down, poppet," he says, his breaths rushing over his lips.

"Cillian," I whisper, too afraid to speak louder.

"Stay down," he repeats, and then the car slams into something before it comes to a skidding stop.

The noise of gunfire is so loud, it fills my ears until all that's left is a ringing noise.

Cillian grabs hold of his gun and opens the door. He rushes out of the car and begins to shoot at the men attacking us.

Unable to stay down, I crawl from the foot space and over the console onto the driver's seat. "Cillian," I whisper again, and it makes his eyes dart to me.

Instead of his usual lopsided grin, a dark grimace distorts his face as he rushes back to me.

"You're safe now." Slipping his hands under my arms, he pulls me out of the car, and then he begins to run with me. "I've got you, poppet. You're going to be okay."

From over his shoulder, I take in the scenery that looks like a war zone. "Cillian," I whisper, terrified and heartbrokenly. Tears flood my eyes, blurring my sight.

"Winter!" I hear Dad shout.

"She's been shot," Cillian yells. "Get me a first aid kit."

It's only then I become aware of the blood dampening my shirt.

My eyes begin to grow heavy as my body jerks with every step Cillian runs. My tongue becomes heavy, and I'm unable to tell him I'll be okay.

It feels as if my heartbeat is slowing down as if the sorrow engulfing me is drowning it. I'm being sucked into a nightmare there's no waking from.

My ears still ring, and I feel wet as if I've been bathed in blood. My mother's. My own.

Cillian lies me down, and then he begins to work on my neck. For a moment, his eyes lock with mine. "I'll fix you, poppet."

Tears warm my icy skin, and the last thing I'm aware of before I pass out is Dad letting out a heartbreaking cry while Cillian works to stop the blood seeping from my neck.

The Past - 14 Years Old.

Since the attack, we've been stuck on a lake island in Finland. There's no more private school. No shopping trips. No interacting with other kids my age.

Since Mom was killed, there's only the island, the guards, and private tutors.

It feels like I'm stuck in a bubble that can pop at any moment.

I'm sitting on the shore, throwing pebbles into the water while I stare at the land in the distance. It harbors the nearest town to us. I've never been there, though.

Letting out a miserable sigh, my thoughts turn to the past. It's been a year since Mom was killed. I got shot in the neck but was lucky. The bullet didn't hit anything vital.

I hear movement behind me, and without glancing over my shoulder, I know it's Cillian. A couple of seconds later, his shadow falls over me, and he grumbles, "You know you shouldn't be out here. Let's head back."

Another heavy sigh escapes me as I throw the last pebble into the water before climbing to my feet.

When I turn around, Cillian tilts his head and lifts his hand to the side of my neck. Caringly, his palm covers the scar. "What can I do to make you smile again?"

He's asked the question many times before, and once again, I can only shrug.

It doesn't feel like I'll ever smile again. Not with Mom gone. She was the heart of our family, and since her death, we've all become zombies, just getting through every day as best we can.

Cillian pulls me into a hug and murmurs, "I wish I could make you feel better, poppet."

Since the shooting, Cillian's become more than just my guard. He's the only friend I have now. Because he was there, he's also the only one I can talk to about my fears and sorrow.

Dad and Sean suffered their own losses, and I don't want to saddle Dad with my miserable feelings whenever he's home from his business trips. Sean's four years younger than me, so I have to be a strong big sister for him.

The thought makes me pull back from Cillian so I can look up at him. He looks like a scary version of Colin Farrell, tall, dark, and always dressed in a suit.

But instead of being afraid of him, he's the only person I feel safe with.

"There is something you can do for me," I whisper, hoping he won't say no.

The creases around his eyes deepen as the corner of his mouth lifts slightly. "Just name it, poppet."

"Teach me how to shoot a gun and how to fight."

A frown forms between Cillian's blue eyes, but after a couple of seconds of thinking about my request, he nods. "If that's what you want."

"I need to be able to protect Sean," I give him my reason, and it makes the lopsided smile I've grown fond of over the years, stretch over his face.

"You're right," he agrees as he slips his arm around my shoulders. We begin to walk, then Cillian says, "First, I'll teach you how to fight. We'll leave learning how to shoot a gun for when you're a little older."

I know it won't be of any use to argue with Cillian. He never says anything he doesn't mean, and there's no changing his mind. With Cillian, what you see, is what you get.

"Okay." I feel a flicker of excitement for the first time since the shooting and ask, "What will you show me first?"

"How to throw a decent punch."

The corner of my mouth lifts slightly, and Cillian notices it. He tugs me closer to his side, then whispers, "I've missed that smile."

Glancing up at the man who saved my life, my smile grows. "Thank you for always being here for me."

For a moment, he gives me a sideways hug. "There's nowhere else I'd rather be, poppet." Cillian's the only one who calls me poppet, and honestly, in some ways, he's the most important person in my life. I love my father and brother, but Cillian's the only one I can lean on.

It's like he filled the empty space in my heart Mom left behind.

"Love you, Cillian," the words fall easily over my lips.

"Ditto, poppet. Ditto."

Chapter 2

DAMIEN

The Past - 18 Years Old.
Zashchitnik.

I've been raised in a family of elite protectors. *Defenders. Custodians. Guardians.* We go by many names, but the official title for the job we do is Custodian.

Watching my older brother, Demitri, graduate from St. Monarch's as a custodian for Alexei Koslov fills my chest with pride. I use the term graduate loosely. The bidding night is kept secret until twenty-four hours before the ceremony takes place.

The Koslov family placed the highest bid for Demitri, which will serve as my brother's first payment for his services. It's the only time we don't have a choice. We have to be paired with the highest bidder. Not that it's a problem. Alexei was determined to have Demitri as his custodian, and he paid five million euros to ensure he got him.

Glancing at Alexei's younger brother, Carson, I mutter, "You better bid double that for me."

Carson lets out a chuckle. "If you're better than Demitri, then I will."

That will happen in five years. We can only attend St. Monarch's once we turn twenty-one.

Demitri and Alexei walk to where we're sitting, and it makes us rise to our feet. I envelop my brother in a hug and murmur, "I'm proud of you."

Demitri has ranked as the best custodian, setting new records in fighting and weaponry. It's my goal to beat them.

Demitri pats my back, and pulling away, his eyes meet mine. "This weekend, we celebrate."

It will be my last weekend with Demitri as he and Alexei are leaving for New York on Monday. There's a sad twinge that mixes with the pride I feel for him, but I shove it aside, knowing it has to be done. We're adults now, which means our lives will take us down different paths.

I shake Alexei's hand to congratulate him, and then we leave St. Monarch's. As we reach the armored jeep and Alexei walks to the driver's side, I ask, "Why doesn't Demitri drive?"

My brother opens the passenger door, then explains, "I need my hands free, so I can shoot anyone who threatens Alexei."

"Oh." Nodding, I climb into the back.

Alexei starts the car, then adds, "You'll learn everything when you start with training."

I wish I was twenty-one already. I can't wait to become as good or better than my brother.

Alexei drives us to a gentlemen's club in Geneva. When we walk into the building, my eyes dart around, drinking in the luxurious interior. Dark wooden furniture is complemented with chrome furnishings. The smell of cigar smoke hangs thick in the air, sweet and robust.

Uncle Michail and Mr. Koslov took Demitri and Alexei to their first gentlemen's club when they turned eighteen. It's a longstanding family tradition.

Until yesterday, I've lived a secluded life at my family's compound situated in Russia. I've learned everything there was to learn about all the fighting styles, and handling different weapons. I also had to become well acquainted with other countries' diverse cultures, especially America, Switzerland, England, and some parts of Africa. I had to learn to speak without a Russian accent as well. It kept me busy, but now I'm ready for more. I hunger for adventure and creating a name for myself as the best custodian.

My gaze goes to Carson. We've exchanged text messages, but living in different countries, we haven't met in person until yesterday. Friends are hard to come by in our world, but like Demitri and Alexei got along right from the start, Carson and I immediately clicked.

Carson's eyes meet mine, the corner of his mouth lifting. "Hopefully, that will be us in five years," he mutters as he gestures at our brothers.

"It better be," I chuckle right before we take a seat at a table.

Alexei places an order for a bottle of vodka with four shot glasses, then he grins at Carson. "Today, I'll make a man of you."

Carson lets out a disgruntled sound through his nose. "I'm already a man."

A server places a bottle of Stoli down in the middle of the table. While Alexei pours us each a glass, he chuckles, "You're not a man until you've gotten drunk and made a woman orgasm." He places a drink in front of Carson. "Until then, you're a kid."

Demitri hands me a shot glass, then asks, "Are you ready to become a man?"

I let out a soft chuckle. "Stupid question."

My first time having sex, and every time after, was with Irina, one of the maids working at the compound. She's taught me everything I know about pleasing a woman.

"Na zdoróv'je," we toast as we lift the drinks to our mouths. The vodka stings my throat as I swallow it down.

Alexei's phone beeps, and after he checks the message, he mutters, "Everything is set for New York."

"The Ruin?" I ask. It's what the hub for illegal activity in Desolation, New York, is called. Once Carson and I are done with St. Monarch's, it will probably be our first destination as well.

Alexei nods as he fills our glasses again. "We have a meeting there."

"Your first contract?" Carson asks as he picks up his drink.

I down mine before settling my eyes on Alexei as he answers, "Yes."

When he doesn't say anything else, my gaze flicks to Demitri, who shakes his head at me so I won't ask more questions regarding their work.

"Drink up," Alexei grumbles.

After the third shot, I start to feel hot under the collar, and by the fifth, my mind starts to grow cloudy.

"You need to practice shooting every second you can," Alexei says to Carson, who just nods in response.

"And you," Demitri says as he locks eyes with me, "you better train every day. Don't embarrass me when you start at St. Monarch's."

"Of course," I mutter as I bring the tumbler to my lips again.

Alexei gestures around the table with his drink. "Don't trust anyone but the men seated at this table."

Both Carson and I nod.

Once we've finished the bottle of vodka, Demitri gets up, which has the rest of us rising to our feet. "Now for the test."

"Test?" I ask, doing my best to not stagger like a drunken fool as we walk deeper into the club.

Demitri and Alexei don't explain what the test entails, and it has Carson and I exchanging a worried look.

They better not expect us to shoot someone. I won't be able to aim straight with all the liquor flooding my veins.

We're led down a hallway, the carpet a deep burgundy beneath our feet. Alexei drags Carson into a room, and I follow Demitri into another room.

A woman stands up from where she was sitting on a bed. Her eyes glide hungrily over me, which makes one of my eyebrows rise.

"Is this the test?" I ask.

"This is Leoni. I picked her myself for you." Demitri's eyes lock with mine. "You have to make her come. Don't leave this room until you're successful," Demitri orders, and then he walks out.

I watch my brother shut the door behind himself before I turn back to Leoni.

The smile is still around her lips. I haven't seen many whores, if that's what Leoni is. She doesn't look like one, with her blonde hair, amber eyes, and delicate pale skin.

I have no intention of failing. It will be an embarrassment I'll never live off.

Determined, I close the distance between us. Leoni tilts her head back as I stop a couple of inches from her. For a moment, our eyes lock, and then I mutter, "Take off your clothes."

I watch as she undresses, and when she steps out of her panties, I grow hard at the sight of her naked body.

"Lie back on the bed," I order, which she immediately does.

Still dressed in my three-piece suit, I crawl over her body. When Leoni reaches for my belt, I shake my head. "Don't move."

Stilling beneath me, heat warms her eyes, and it makes the corner of my mouth lift.

Irina was right. Women love men who take charge.

It doesn't take me long to get Leoni ready for me, and after I've slipped on a condom, I take her hard and fast, which has her screaming her orgasm for all to hear.

My own pleasure fades as quickly as it came, and after I've disposed of the condom, I fix my clothes before leaving Leoni naked and breathless on the bed.

I walk back to the table where Demitri and Alexei are waiting. Not seeing Carson, the corner of my mouth lifts with a victorious feeling.

I take my seat and picking up the shot in front of me, I down it before I lock eyes with my brother.

"Good," he murmurs, pride shining from his eyes. "What did you learn?"

Shaking my head, I let out a chuckle. "It's easy to satisfy a woman?"

"What else?" Demitri asks. When I shrug, he leans his elbows on the dark wood, his eyes locking with mine. "That's the closest you will ever get to a woman. If you marry, it's to strengthen your footing in The Ruin. There's no place for love in our world. Your loyalty will always belong to the one you guard, which means he or she will own your heart, your soul, and your body."

Carson sits down next to me and turning my gaze to him, I grumble, "I understand."

That person will be Carson Koslov. When my time comes, I'll be loyal to him, and only him.

Chapter 3

WINTER

The Present – Winter 21; Damien 23.

"I don't want you to go," Sean says for the hundredth time as we step out of the mansion. My gaze goes to where our father talks with Cillian and the rest of the security team, who will escort me to the private airport.

Sean, my younger brother, has made his feelings abundantly clear. I wish he would understand I'm doing this for him. He'll turn eighteen in a year, and then it's expected of him to follow in our father's footsteps. Sean will take over our diamond smuggling business, and someone has to protect him. That someone will be me because I won't trust anyone else with Sean's life.

When I turned sixteen, I learned the Hemsley clan owns Angola, Sierra Leone, the DRC, Ivory Coast, and Zimbabwe. Africa's diamonds belong to us, which has placed a hefty target on our heads. It's the reason our mother was assassinated, and I took a bullet to my neck, which is why the family business means so much to me. I've bled for it, and I won't let anyone take it away from us.

Turning my gaze back to Sean, I say, "It's only for two years. Keep your head low while I'm gone."

I wish I could take him with me to St. Monarch's. It's the only place on this goddamn earth that's neutral ground. I need the training. I have to become the best for Sean. I just hate leaving him behind.

"Stay," he begs, giving me a pleading look I usually can't resist.

Taking a step forward, I lift my hands to his shoulders and lock eyes with him. "Listen to me, Sean. It's only for two years. I need the training. While I'm gone, you have to be extra careful. Don't leave the grounds unless you really have to. Always keep the guards with you and wear your bulletproof vest. Once I'm back, I'll make it up to you."

Frustration tightens his features. "I don't care about that. I don't want you to go. We shouldn't split up. There's a target on your head as well."

I give my brother a comforting smile as I pull him into a hug. "I can take care of myself, and Cillian will be with me. Don't worry."

Sean's arms wrap around me, and he clings to me as if he has the power to keep me here. "Please, don't go," he whispers, his voice tight with worry.

"Shh... I'll be fine. Just take care of yourself. Okay?"

Sean nods, his grip on me tightening even more.

We both have our mother's red hair and green eyes, but Sean got our father's large build and strong features. He went through a growth spurt last year, shooting well past me. I, on the other hand, got our mother's petite frame. At twenty-one, I still look younger than Sean even though I'm four years older than him.

When we pull apart, Sean shakes his head. "I have a bad feeling."

"Nothing's going to happen to me. St. Monarch's is safe. Stop worrying, please."

"It's time," Father says as he steps closer to us.

Nodding, I stand on my toes and press a farewell kiss to Sean's cheek. "Keep your head down and stay on the grounds," I remind him again.

He nods, taking a step back, frustration still tightening his features.

Father pulls me into a hug, then whispers, "You don't have to do this."

"I know." I rest my cheek against his chest. "I want to. For Sean. For you."

Father nods as he pulls back, his eyes drifting over my face. The corner of his mouth lifts. "Cillian will be stationed outside the grounds. Don't hesitate to call him if anything happens."

I step back, and with love filling my heart, I look at the two men in my life. "You both worry too much. I can take care of myself."

Father lets out a chuckle. "We should protect you, not the other way around."

"No," I grin at them. "You run the business, and I'll keep you safe. That's the end of the discussion."

Father's eyes lock with mine as they turn dark. "You're the Blood Princess of the Hemsley clan. Never forget that."

"I won't, Father," I promise. Turning away from them, I climb into the back of the armored jeep. My personal firearm, a Heckler and Koch, digs into my lower back, but I ignore the slight discomfort. I also have a Glock strapped to my ankle.

Before Cillian shuts the door, I look at my father and brother. "I love you both with all my heart."

Sean's eyes begin to redden with unshed tears. "Love you too."

Father's mouth tips up with a proud smile. "Love you, my princess. Call me the instant you're safely at the St. Monarch's."

I nod as the door shuts, and then I focus on taking deep breaths because I can't cry. This was my decision. I've learned all there is to learn from my private lessons with Cillian. Now I need to train with the best because they're the ones who will come after my family.

For two years, I'll live with my enemies. I'll watch. I'll learn. I will show them I'm a threat, and they will fear me.

For Sean. For Father. For our family business.

While we drive to the private airstrip where the jet is waiting to take me to Switzerland, I stare down at my hands.

I feel Cillian's gaze on me, and forcing a smile to my lips, I lift my head to look at him. He gives me a lopsided grin, but it's tainted by the worry he feels about me leaving home. "Remember there are six syndicate groups. The Custodians, consisting of the best protectors. You'll train with them."

I nod. "My goal is to break Demitiri Vetrov's records."

Demitri became a legend during his time at St. Monarch's. Now he protects the top assassin in the world, Alexei Koslov, making them an unbeatable team. I need to be better than them because right now, we don't stand a chance if they are hired to come after us. The thought makes my jaw clench and my top lip curl up.

Cillian nods, then he continues, "It's not going to be easy. It's going to hurt because none of the custodians in training will hold back just because you're a woman. They all have the same goal. To become the best."

I swallow hard, fear slithering into my heart. I have no idea what to expect.

Cillian's eyes darken with worry as he says, "The other five syndicates consist of Arms, Assassins, Smugglers, Cartels, and the Bravta. Only the wealthiest crime families get to attend, so they can cultivate the specific set of skills needed to run their family businesses. There's only one rule – no killing. So at least there's that."

I nod while memorizing everything he's telling me. After all, knowledge is power.

When the jeep stops right by the private jet, I wait for Cillian to open my door. My eyes continuously scan over my surroundings as I step out of the vehicle, and I tug at the bulletproof vest that's tightly wrapped around my chest. It matches my black pants and boots, which I like to think of as my combat outfit. I want to dress up as much as the next girl, but that's only for special occasions.

My spine is stiff as I ascend the stairs with Cillian right behind me. Once I'm safely inside the plane, I let out a breath of relief.

Six hours and I'll enter the safety of St. Monarch's. A lot can happen in six hours, but at least I have Cillian with me.

Pulling the gun from behind my back, I set it down on the seat beside me. I unstrap the vest and take a deep breath as I place it next to my firearm. Cillian does the same where he's seated across from me.

"Are you sure, poppet?" he asks.

Our eyes meet, and knowing it's useless trying to hide my feelings from him, I say, "Even though I'm terrified of the unknown, I have to do it."

"I'll be right outside St. Monarch's," he assures me again. Our guards aren't allowed on the premises. I guess it's to ensure everyone's safety.

This time a genuine smile tugs at my mouth. "Yeah, at least I'll have you there."

As the jet begins to move, I lean my head back and stare out the window.

It's just two years, Winter. You have to do this for your family.

DAMIEN

Standing in my personal quarters, I cross my arms over my chest as I watch everyone arrive.

St. Monarch's has been my home for the past twenty-two months. As the best protector in training, I will be paired with the top assassin when I graduate. I won't settle for anyone else but Carson. It's my only goal. The bidding date hasn't been announced yet, though, and I'm growing impatient to be free of this place.

I watch as Adrian Vincent climbs out of his armored jeep. He's Carson's competition and probably the first one I'll kill the instant we step outside the gates of St. Monarch's. There are four assassins in training right now, and they're taught to live by a code – don't kill for sport.

But Adrian's different. I see the thirst for blood in his eyes. It's not about the money for him. Once he starts killing, it will be for pleasure, and he'll try to take out the competition first. He's arrogant enough to believe he could actually succeed in killing Carson.

Another armored jeep pulls up, and I watch as an older man climbs out of the driver's side. He walks around the vehicle to open the passenger door for someone. A flash of red draws my attention, and then my gaze locks on the woman getting out of the jeep. St. Monarch's only allows you to attend once you're over twenty-one, so she must be of age even though she looks younger.

When the woman turns around and stares up at the windows, my gaze narrows. *Winter Hemsley*. She's even more beautiful than I heard.

The man, who's probably her personal guard, says something to her, and it makes her smile. I watch as they hug each other, and then she takes a couple of steps away from the jeep as her guard climbs back in the vehicle to leave.

Winter moves with grace, and my eyes take in her petite curves, clearly visible under the tight-fitting black pants and shirt, before settling on her face again.

Her gaze sweeps over the buildings and grounds, on guard and ready to defend herself should a threat appear.

The sight of her makes my heartbeat speed up a little, and it has the corner of my mouth curving up. Not many women manage to elicit any kind of emotion in me. Then again, Winter Hemsley is no ordinary woman. She's the

Blood Princess. One of the heirs to the Hemsley's smuggling empire. Her grandfather orchestrated the massacre of many villages in Africa. Ruthlessness runs in her veins.

A merciless beauty radiates from her, designed to bring men to their knees for her to walk over, using them as stepping stones in her climb to the top.

Another car pulls up, which belongs to Vince Blanco. I tilt my head as I watch the two enemies come face to face. The Blanco family had Rose Hemsley, Winter's mother, assassinated. Winter was also shot during the attack, and the Hemsley family has lived in hiding ever since.

But still, here she is. The breathtakingly beautiful Blood Princess who survived an assassination attempt. It's a rare sight indeed.

Winter and Vince lock eyes, and I'm surprised when Vince is the first to walk away. It looks like he's chuckling.

Winter's gaze follows Vince until he enters the building, and the hatred turning her face to stone makes a smile form around my lips. She's got fire. I'll give her that.

I keep watching as one armored jeep after the other pulls up. Hours later, when the last attendee has arrived, I turn away from the window, not happy that twenty-one people will be attending St. Monarch's. I'm going to miss the peace and quiet from when it was just nine of us. Hopefully, I won't be here for much longer.

There's still three hours until Madame Keller, the architect of St. Monarch's, gives the welcome speech at dinner. Grabbing my hand tape, I walk out of my room and start to wrap the fabric around my fingers, palms, and wrists. I don't look up as I make my way to the gym.

Soft murmurs fill the hallways as all the new attendees make their way to their assigned quarters. St. Monarch's used to be a castle built in the late seventeen hundreds. It's situated right outside Geneva, and although the furnishings have been renovated, the wooden floors creak with every step.

I walk to the back of the academy and enter the last sparring studio at the end of the hallway. There are a couple so we can have privacy when we train. Growing up, I've learned every fighting style known to mankind. I've spent the past eighteen months creating my own combination, taking moves from Muay Thai, Krav Maga, Kung Fu, and wrestling.

Removing my earphones from my pocket, I'm just about to put them in when I feel eyes on me. Glancing over my shoulder, my gaze connects with Paulie's. Paul Connor will probably end up working with Winter Hemsley, seeing as they're both Irish.

"Did you even go home?" Paulie asks as he steps into the room.

"No." After my uncle joined Demitri in America, there's nothing to go home to.

I watch as he wraps his hands, then he grins at me. "Take it easy on me."

I turn my body to face him. "There's no such thing as easy in our world."

Paulie lets out a chuckle. "Fine. Just don't break anything."

"You should fight Hugo," I say. I actually like the Irishman.

"He's not here yet." Paulie begins to circle me. "Come on. Teach me something."

Slowly, I shake my head. "You know that's not how it works." Paulie starts to jump lightly, and it has me adding, "Take the out I'm giving you, Paulie."

"I'll fight," a woman's voice comes from behind us, and it has our heads snapping in the direction of the door.

"As I live and breathe," Paulie chuckles. "The Blood Princess in the flesh."

She's even smaller and more stunning up close. Her creamy white skin makes her red hair look dark, and the fierce expression in her eyes has them sparkling like emeralds.

With the full intention of finding another empty studio where I can train, I begin to walk toward her.

"You're leaving?" Paulie asks.

"It's crowded," I mutter as the side of my body bumps against Winter's when I pass by her. To my surprise, she doesn't stagger backward, and a spark jumps between us.

"Or just afraid to get your ass kicked by a woman," she says, an edge to her voice making it sound like a warning.

Stopping in the hallway, I take a deep breath before I glance over my shoulder. Our eyes lock, and for a moment, heat sizzles between us.

I wonder if she's as feisty between the sheets.

She doesn't look away, but instead, her gaze narrows on me as if she can read my mind.

Deciding to teach her a lesson, I murmur, "If you can beat Paulie, I'll consider fighting you."

Chapter 4

WINTER

My eyebrows lift as I point over my shoulder at the guy standing in the studio. "Is that Paulie?"

The man who was about to leave nods. My gaze drifts over his body that looks like a lethal weapon, his muscles tense as if he's ready to attack at any moment. Bringing my eyes back to his face, I take in his chiseled jaw, his sharp cheekbones, and then his dark eyes. There's no emotion in them.

Everything about this man screams danger, and it makes a shiver crawl down my spine. Still, he's the most beautiful man I've ever laid eyes on.

"Don't go anywhere. This won't take long," I say, the corner of my mouth lifting with confidence, but all I get in return is an impassive expression, and for some reason, it only makes him look hotter.

I walk toward Paulie, the guy I'll fight first. He's shorter than the other man, with a broader chest. His stocky build will make him slow. I can use that to my advantage.

Glancing at the door, I notice the other man leaning against the doorjamb, crossing his arms over his chest. It makes the toned muscles and veins in his arms prominent and hard to ignore.

Danger has never looked so attractive before.

Paulie tosses me the hand wrap, and I quickly cover my palms and fingers with it.

When I'm ready, Paulie gives me a toothy grin as if he's already won the fight, then he chuckles, "Unlike Damien, I'll take it easy on you, Princess."

Damien?

Damien who?

"Remind me to thank you once I've won," I reply, my lips curving slightly.

We begin to circle each other, and I keep my body relaxed while holding my hands up in front of me.

Paulie takes a jab at me, but I duck and avoid the blow easily. Wanting to end this fight so I can face off with Damien, I dart forward, and grabbing hold of Paulie's shoulders, I deliver a double-flying knee kick to his chin. Paulie falls backward on his ass ending the fight.

"Thanks for taking it easy on me," I say to Paulie before turning my head to Damien.

"You okay, Paulie?" Damien asks as he steps back into the studio, his muscles rippling under his golden skin.

"Yeah," Paulie mutters as he climbs to his feet. "Just embarrassed."

"Damien?" I ask, tilting my head.

"Really?" Paulie gasps, surprise flashing over his face as he wipes the blood from his busted lip. "You don't know who Damien is? Have you been living under a rock?"

No, just a secluded island. I shrug. "Let's pretend I have."

"Damien Vetrov," Damien says, his voice filled with pride and warning.

My eyes snap to his face as shock vibrates through me. "Demitri Vetrov's brother?"

"The one and only," Paulie answers.

Oh, God.

Damien's stare is sharp and intense, closely watching my reaction to finding out who he is.

Fear trickles through my veins, and I pray to all that's holy, it doesn't show on my face.

Cillian told me for generations, the Vetrovs have raised the elite of the elite when it comes to protectors. He spoke of them as if they're gods. I have no doubt Damien will end up being just as good as his older brother, Demitri.

'Unkillable, merciless, with a devastating potency no one can escape.'

Cillian's words vibrate through me as Damien comes to stand opposite me. Knowing who he is, makes his body seem like an unstoppable force of nature.

Shit. I'm about to get my ass kicked.

Stupid, Winter. Next time make sure who your opponent is before you throw down the gauntlet to fight.

If Cillian was here, he'd scold me for making such a stupid mistake. But he also taught me backing down from a fight is worse than losing. I roll my shoulders to loosen my muscles and mutter, "Let's do this."

Damien's penetrating gaze lazily sweeps over me as if I'm a waste of his time. When he doesn't make any effort to move, I narrow my eyes at him and dart forward. He brings up his left arm, thwarting my blow, and then his right hand shoots out.

His strong fingers clamp around my throat, and when his grip on my neck tightens, I know what's coming. I brace myself as Damien sweeps my legs out from under me, and my back slams into the hard floor with a dull thud.

Grabbing hold of his wrist, I try to buck my body up. Damien moves fast, and with stealthy power, he slips under me while securing his arm around my neck. His right leg locks both of mine to the floor, and his left arm wraps tightly around my waist, effectively incapacitating me.

His masculine scent folds around me, only making me more aware of the brutal power surrounding me. I should fight back, but for the first time in my life, I'm overwhelmed by a man.

This is nothing like when I'm sparring with Cillian.

Suddenly Damien shoves me off him, and my body rolls to the side. "You're no match for me, Princess," he hisses.

Picking myself up off the floor, my eyes burn into Damien's broad back as he stalks out of the room. Formidable strength and danger emanate off him, serving as a constant warning.

Shit, I don't stand a chance against him.

I've never seen any of the Vetrovs up close, so coming face to face with the youngest one is startling, to say the least. Life has taught me the most exquisite things in life are the deadliest, and Damien's too attractive, too strong, and too much of a threat.

Worried about what this means, I pull the wrap off my hands and toss it aside, my breaths rushing over my lips.

Shit. Shit. Shit.

Not only is Damien good, but he's... attractive in a way that demands your admiration. It's too disarming, and I can't allow myself to be distracted while I'm here. It's a huge problem, and I don't know how to deal with it.

Then another thought enters my mind. Damien could've hurt me, but he didn't. I know the Vetrovs live by a code. They only kill to protect whomever they're loyal to, and that might be my only saving grace right now.

But once Damien graduates and he's paired with an assassin, I'll have both him and Demitri to worry about. And the assassins they're guarding.

God.

"Don't feel bad. Damien's the best. He's broken all of Demitri's records," Paulie says, reminding me he's still in the room.

My eyes flick to him before I walk toward the door.

"Nice meeting you, Princess," Paulie calls after me as I turn into the hallway.

I knew it wouldn't be easy attending St. Monarch's. Still, nothing prepared me for coming face to face with Vince Blanco... and Damien Vetrov on my first day here.

The Blanco family had my mother killed and tried but failed to kill me. All to send my father a message. They want Africa.

It's going to be near impossible to watch Vince Blanco laugh… breathe… and not try to kill him.

And Damien?

The blood flowing through my veins warms just at the mere thought of him.

I head up the stairs to get to my quarters, my eyes continually scanning over my surroundings. As I climb the last couple of stairs, I come to a sudden halt. Standing in the middle of the hallway are Damien Vetrov and Carson Koslov. They're giving each other a brotherly hug.

The spit dries in my mouth at the sight.

Holy mother of saints.

Fear soaks into my bones. If they're paired and team up with their brothers, my family and I are as good as dead once someone hires them to assassinate us.

Carson has the same blond hair as his brother, and when his dark eyes flick to me, it sends a chill rushing over my body. Vigilant and deadly.

Slowly he tilts his head, the corner of his mouth twitching. "Winter Hemsley." His low voice makes my name sound like a warning.

'Show no fear,' I hear Cillian's voice in my mind.

Lifting my chin, I lock eyes with him. "Carson Koslov."

The corner of his mouth twitches again. "Not what I expected a princess to look like."

Wanting to make a statement, I lift my hand and brush my hair back over my shoulder, so the scar on my neck is clearly visible.

"I'm no ordinary princess," I murmur.

I begin to walk again, my gaze moving from Carson to Damien as I pass right through the middle of them. For a moment, pressure builds, and I'm inundated by the testosterone coming off them in waves.

Show no Fear. Not ever.

I keep my chin high, and when I reach my quarters, I take hold of the doorknob and glance back at the men. They're both watching me, probably sizing me up.

Pushing the door open, I step inside. I lock it behind me and then let out a breath of relief.

Instead of crumbling in fear, it only makes me more determined to become the best. I have two years to train in combat and armory.

Walking to my bedroom, I pick up my bag, and pulling my phone out, I dial my father's number. I already called him to tell him I arrived safely, but now I need to warn them.

"Twice in one day. Do you miss us already?" Father's warm voice comes over the line.

"Carson Koslov and Damien Vetrov," I get right to the point. "It seems they're already pairing up."

"Fuck," Father hisses. "You saw this with your own eyes?"

"Yes." I take a trembling breath. "Go back into hiding. I need to know you and Sean are safe until I'm done with my training."

"I'll send more guards for you," Father says.

"I won't step off the grounds. Don't worry about me. I have Cillian. You need to leave as soon as possible. Let me know when you reach the island."

The island's not easily accessible. Any plane, helicopter, or boat can be taken out before they reach land. Right now, it's the safest place for them.

"We'll leave within the hour. I'll send out a tracker to watch Alexei Koslov and Demitri Vetrov. As soon as they move in our direction, I'll alert you. It will be better for you to join us then."

"They won't try anything at St. Monarch's. No one dares the risk of being banned," I remind Father. Being banned comes with a steep price on your head. An open contract that will have every assassin in the world coming after you. "The Koslov and Vetrov families have honor. They'll wait until I leave the academy. I'll see the rest of the attendees at dinner tonight. I'll notify you if there are other families we should be keeping an eye on."

"Do that." Father clears his throat.

"Let me know as soon as you reach the island," I remind him.

"I will. Stay safe, my princess."

"You too, Father."

We end the call, and I quickly dial Cillian's number.

"Poppet?" he answers, his voice tight with worry.

"I'm fine. I'm just calling to let you know Damien Vetrov and Carson Koslov are here."

"Fuck," he spits the word over the line.

"Be careful," I warn him.

"I will."

"I have to get ready for dinner."

Cillian lets out a heavy breath. "Remember, keep your head high and show no fear. I'm right outside St. Monarch's."

I nod. "Vince Blanco is also here. I didn't tell father."

Another curse escapes Cillian. "Christ, poppet."

"I'll be okay," I try to ease his worry. I lick my lips before I continue, "But the moment we leave St. Monarch's, I want him dead."

"Consider it a graduation present," Cillian promises.

"Stay safe," I murmur before I cut the call, and knowing I only have an hour and a half left to prepare for dinner, I run myself a bath.

Tonight I get to dress up. I've picked a light gray dress with a heart-shaped bodice. The top layer of chiffon shimmers, reminding me of diamonds, and the bottom layer is stained red. That's why I chose it. Tonight I'll be the proud Blood Princess, here to remind my enemies I've survived death once, and I can do it again.

I'm not some weak girl they can swat out of the way. Never. I'm a fierce woman with Hemsley blood running through my veins. I'm a force to be reckoned with because I have too much to lose.

DAMIEN

Dressed in a black tuxedo, I let out a sigh as I leave my room. I'm not in the mood for this dinner, but it's obligatory.

Another door opens down the hallway, and I glance in its direction. I suck in a sharp breath at the sight of Winter Hemsley. She looks absolutely breathtaking, her hair curled and pinned back with a diamond comb. The moment she starts walking toward me, the dress moves, and I get glimpses of red as the fabric swishes at her feet.

She keeps impressing me. First with her fighting skills when she dropped Paulie in eight seconds, then wearing her scar like a warning to all that she's a survivor. Now elegance and pride exude from her with every step she takes. It makes her irresistible.

Winter lifts her chin, once again giving me a view of the scar on her neck. Her eyes lock on mine, and when she's only a couple of steps away, she murmurs, "Thinking of how you're going to kill me, Vetrov?"

It doesn't escape my attention that she didn't say *try* to kill her, which means I'm the biggest threat in her eyes.

"You'll be here for a couple of years. I don't plan that far ahead." I let my eyes drift over her body before bringing them back to hers. "For now, I'll admire the view."

She stops in front of me, the corner of her mouth lifting. "Care to show me the way?"

Clever girl.

If I agree, it will show the other families I'm giving her the time of day. They'll think twice about coming after her because they'll think I'm her ally.

I shouldn't waste a second of my time on her, but I still find myself nodding. Winter links her arm through mine, resting her palm on my forearm. Instantly her touch sends a spark through my arm.

As we begin to walk, I shorten my strides to match hers while dismissing the obvious attraction I feel toward her.

"Paulie says you're the best. You've beaten your brother's records?" Winter's voice is nothing but a soft hum, threatening to spin a web around us.

"I have," I murmur, keeping my own voice low.

"And you'll be paired with Carson Koslov?" she asks another question.

This time I only nod as I realize what she's doing. Keep your friends close but keep your enemies closer. This is a strategic move on her part and has nothing to do with making a statement to the other attendees.

I'm the enemy she fears most.

Turning my head, I lower my eyes to her face. It only takes a second before she glances up, and our gazes lock. We come to a stop at the top of the stairs, and an uncanny anticipation begins to sizzle to life between us. Whether it's because of the physical attraction or a predator setting sights on its prey, I don't know yet.

Winter pulls her arm free from mine as she lifts her chin a little higher. "I'm here to train as a custodian for my family. I'll protect them."

My eyebrow rises slightly. "You think you can compete against me?"

Her lips curl up in a beautiful smile that has my eyes lowering to them. Full and red, like a strawberry that's ripe for the picking. "I'm not here to compete," she replies to my question. My gaze snaps back up to hers as she adds, "I'm here to become the best."

My eyes narrow on her, and even though she's acting brave, the fear trembling in her green irises tells me a different story. I can't help but smile at her boldness. "Good luck."

"Flirting with death again, Hemsley?"

I watch as all emotion drains from Winter's face before she turns to look at Vince Blanco. She keeps her body positioned sideways, so her back isn't turned to me.

Winter again impresses me as she scoffs at Vince. "The assassins your family sent missed."

Vince takes a threatening step toward her, a scowl narrowing his eyes. "Your mother is a rotting corpse. I'd say the bullet hit the target."

Fire sparks to life in Winter's gaze. She closes the last of the distance between her and Vince, and even though she has to tilt her head back to look up at him, she seems a million times more powerful than him.

"Enjoy life while you have the protection of these walls," she hisses at him. Winter's eyes stay locked on his as if she's daring him to make a move right here. But he won't. Vince is not a fighter.

Again Vince is the first to look away. He steps back then moves around Winter, bumping his shoulder against hers as he heads for the stairs.

I watch as she takes a deep breath, and ignoring me, she follows after Vince toward the banquet hall.

The first thing Demitri taught me was to never let anyone in, to never indulge in relationships. My loyalty belongs to the person I'll guard – Carson.

Up until now, it hasn't been a problem. But as I watch Winter glide over the polished floor, the desire returns.

Shaking my head and shoving the attraction I feel toward Winter aside, I take the stairs down to the lower floor.

Carson is all that matters, and if he gets the contract to kill the Hemsley's, I'll have to let it happen.

Chapter 5

WINTER

I focus on my breaths as rage and hatred create a storm in my chest. My heart slams against my ribs, making me feel confined in the dress instead of beautiful.

Stepping into the banquet hall, I feel naked without my firearms and combat clothes.

My eyes follow Vince Blanco, my hands itching to strangle the life from him. To him and his family, my beloved mother was nothing but an animal they hunted for sport. It was a senseless killing. The threat didn't make my father hand over the blood diamond business to them.

My mother was kind and caring. She was loved dearly by all our employees. She was angelic, and now she's immortalized in our hearts.

With Cillian's help, I will see Vince Blanco die. I'll see the life drain from his eyes and his blood spill over the ground, just like my mother's.

"If you keep staring, he'll know he managed to get to you," Damien suddenly murmurs next to me. "Never show your enemy they've managed to rattle your cage."

My head snaps up, my gaze colliding with Damien's deadly brown eyes. Again I feel the punch to my stomach from how attractive he is. It's bewildering, to say the least. His dark brown hair looks thick and silky, and the slight stubble on his jaw accentuates his manliness. The tuxedo he's wearing makes him look like a perfect male specimen – nothing short of a god.

If only he wasn't deadly.

"Giving advice to the enemy? Not clever of you," I mutter as I let my gaze sweep over the other attendees. Everyone is scattered, watchful of their enemies.

The Bratva comes in, followed by the Cartels, and it makes my eyebrows lift. Isabella Terrero. Princess of Terror. Like me, she has a nickname seeing as her mother is the Queen of Terror. Only her nickname comes from peddling flesh instead of smuggling blood diamonds.

Another woman comes in, and not recognizing her, I ask Damien, "Who is she?"

"MJ Fang. She's a custodian in training," he informs me with a low rumbling voice.

So I won't be the only woman. Things just got interesting.

My lips curve up at the thought.

"Do you know MJ?" Damien asks, pulling my attention back to him.

"Not personally," I murmur.

He lets out a chuckle, the corner of his mouth curving into a sexy grin that causes a fluttering in my stomach. "Do any of us *really* know each other?"

"I guess not," I murmur, my gaze drinking in his handsome features.

There's nothing wrong with looking.

Damien gestures to a table. "The custodians will all be seated there." He walks away from me, and I take a moment to admire him from behind.

Up until now, the only guy I've been with was one of the guards, Petro. It was nothing but meaningless sex. I haven't dated like other girls my age, and I never will. I'll probably marry whoever my father tells me to marry to secure an alliance.

It doesn't stop me from admiring an attractive male specimen when I see one, and Damien is definitely attractive… and lethal. Such an intoxicating mixture.

Madame Keller comes into the room, followed by her two personal custodians. For a seventy-three-year-old woman, she looks nothing older than fifty. Her grey hair is swept up in a bun, and her makeup's applied with an expert hand. I can't help but admire how successful she's been in creating St. Monarch's.

My eyes move to the custodian's table, and seeing Hugo Lamas seated at it makes my stomach tighten.

God, the competition is brutal.

I walk toward the table where there are three seats open. Not wanting to back down from a threat, I take the chair between Damien and Hugo.

Hugo slowly turns his face to me, and for a split second, our eyes meet before he glances back to Madame Keller. He's indifferent about my being here, and I'm taking it as a good sign. He still has to learn the valuable lesson to never underestimate the competition. Right now, it gives me an advantage over him.

"Welcome," Madame Keller says, and it instantly grows quiet in the room. "We have twelve new attendees. It's the most we've ever hosted. There's only one rule; no killing. You're allowed to conduct business as always. If a fight breaks out, we will not intervene… unless there's a death."

So basically, we can beat each other to a pulp. It's not a comforting thought.

I feel eyes on me, and then my gaze connects with Vince's. Lifting his hand to his neck, he drags a finger over the width, indicating he's planning on killing me.

I'll have to watch my back. Getting hurt means I won't be able to train, and I can't have that.

I glance over the other attendees. Most aren't here to learn their trade but to hide behind the secure walls of St. Monarch's. To them, this place is nothing more than a resort. Other's are here to build alliances, and the rest are probably here for the same reason as me – to learn what I can and show I'm a threat.

"The only weapons on the premises are held in the armory. If a weapon is found on you, the penalty will be severe." Madame Keller's gaze sweeps over all the tables. "St. Monarch's is not responsible for what happens outside our gates. We hope you will find your stay with us a pleasant one."

As soon as Madame Keller takes a seat at the head table upfront, servers flood into the hall.

I look over the instructors. I'm only interested in Miss Dervishi, who'll be training us in weapons, and Mr. Yeoh, who's the martial arts Grandmaster. I'll be spending four hours a day in each class.

Platters of seafood, various meats, and vegetables are placed down in the middle of the table.

A waiter begins to take our drink orders, and when she turns her attention to me, I say, "Cranberry juice. No ice."

"Vodka," Damien murmurs. "Stoli."

It's only when he orders the Russian drink that I hear his accent slip through, and it makes a tingle spiral down my spine.

Turning my head toward Damien, our eyes connect, and for the longest moment, we just stare at each other.

Attraction skirts around the edges of the fear he instills in me, but nothing in this world will make me act on it. I keep staring at him because one, I won't back down, and two, I like admiring masterpieces.

DAMIEN

"Wondering if you can take me on?" I ask, keeping my voice low, so the others seated at the table won't hear.

"No. Just admiring the view," she throws my words from earlier back at me.

The corner of my mouth lifts in a smirk, and it has her eyes lowering to my lips while interest darkens her eyes.

Lust. It's the only other emotion that's as strong as hate.

"Enemies can admire each other," she whispers.

"True," I agree. Tilting my head, I ask, "What have I done to become your enemy?"

She lets out a burst of silent laughter, and it makes her cleavage swell for a tantalizing moment. "It's simple. If you're not for my family, you're against us."

"No neutral ground?"

"Never." With the word drifting over her lips, she turns her attention to the table where the families who deal in arms are seated.

Winter is preparing for war, and I wonder how her father and brother fit into everything. Why did they task her with the defense of the family?

Winter was right when she told Carson she's no ordinary princess. She's the furthest thing from one. *A warrior.*

To get the dinner over with, I plate a couple of slices of beef and some vegetables for myself. Only then do the rest of the table begin to help themselves to food, and it makes my eyes narrow as I glance at each of my companions.

It used to be just Hugo, Paulie, and myself.

My gaze settles on Megan-Joe Fang, also known as MJ. Her father is a retired custodian, so she might be a match for Hugo and Paulie.

As I take the last bite of my meal, I turn my eyes back to Winter. She's shown me she can fight Paulie, but I'm not so sure whether she'll be able to stand her ground against Hugo.

Winter should be sitting with the Smugglers. She's too tiny, too fragile-looking to train with us.

Feeling rattled by the worry slithering through my veins, I down my drink and get up from the chair. Walking away from the table, I feel eyes burning on my back. Those of my enemies, my competition, and then the sensation changes as Winter's eyes settle on me.

Right now, there might be a physical attraction between us, but I'm sure it will die a sudden death when we're forced to fight tomorrow.

Even though training only starts at eight, I'm in the studio to warm up by six every day.

Wearing my usual rashguard shirt and MMA shorts, I strap on the shin guards, hand wrap, and gloves. When I'm ready, I head over to the reflex bag and begin with slow punches, increasing my pace every couple of minutes.

I've just started working up a sweat when I feel the air shift. Glancing over my shoulder, a frown settles on my face when I see Winter walking into the sparring studio. She's tied her hair back in a ponytail, and it makes her look even younger. Then my eyes lower to her body. In the tight black pants and shirt, every curve is on full display.

Once again, I shove the attraction aside, and before continuing to punch the bag, I grumble, "You should join the Smugglers."

"Morning to you too," she mutters.

I'm not one to care about others or to issue warnings, but still, I find myself huffing, "You're going to get hurt."

"Aww, I didn't know you cared," she sasses me.

Shooting her a glare, I see she's busy putting on her gear.

"I don't." The words are clipped. If she doesn't heed the warning, she'll just have to roll with the punches. *Literally.*

I continue with my exercises, doing my best to ignore Winter, where she's jumping rope on the other side of the room.

When the other trainees and Grandmaster Yeoh enter the studio, I stop punching and walk to where I left my bag. I retrieve a water bottle and down half of it before using a towel to wipe the sweat from my face and neck.

"Morning," Grandmaster Yeoh says as he bows slightly.

We return his greeting, then wait for his instructions.

Grandmaster Yeoh's eyes dart between Winter and MJ, then he says, "Let's see what experience the newcomers have. Miss Fang versus..." His eyes jump over us, then he mutters, "Mr. Lamas."

The rest of us move to the back of the studio, and Winter ends up standing between Paulie and me.

"Nothing like an ass-whooping first thing in the morning," Paulie chuckles as MJ and Hugo start to circle each other.

Hugo blows MJ a kiss which makes her attack. She manages to give Hugo an uppercut and a punch to the side of his head before his right fist connects with her left side. It sends her flying to the side and her body sliding over the floor.

Ouch.

I glance down at Winter's face, but instead of seeing fear, she's focused on the fight.

MJ climbs back to her feet, shaking her head. It has Hugo attacking, and my muscles clench when he goes airborne, his body twisting before he delivers a kick to the left side of MJ's head. This time she flies, and when she drops to the floor, she stays down, out cold from the blow.

I expected MJ to be better. Guess I was wrong.

Grandmaster Yeoh slowly shakes his head, then mutters, "Move her to the side so we can continue with the training."

Hugo grabs hold of MJ's arm and drags her to the other side of the room.

"Next," Grandmaster Yeoh snaps. My heartbeat kicks up, hoping Winter will be paired with Paulie. "Miss Hemsley versus..." Grandmaster Yeoh's eyes flick between Paulie and me, and after a couple of seconds, he settles on me. "Mr. Vetrov."

Fuck.

Chapter 6

WINTER

Shit… here goes nothing.

Knowing Damien is stronger than me, I'll just have to make sure he doesn't get a punch in, or I'll probably end up like MJ.

I walk to the middle of the class and watch as Damien unhurriedly moves closer.

Rolling my shoulders, I lift my hands and then keep still, my body tense as I watch him shake his head lightly.

The fact that he's clearly unhappy because he has to fight me makes annoyance trickle through my chest.

"Let's get this over with, Vetrov," I hiss, and it has his eyes locking on mine.

He takes a deep breath then bringing his arms up, he doesn't make fists while assuming a Muay Thai stance.

I assume the same stance, just to show him I have experience in all the fighting styles.

After a couple of seconds of us only staring at each other, Grandmaster Yeoh snaps, "Begin!"

It has me darting forward and bringing my right leg up for a kick to Damien's side, he jumps back before I even manage to get close.

He's faster than me. Shit, I was hoping to have speed on my side.

We circle each other for a moment, and then Damien's right leg comes up, only to connect with my thigh. It has me shooting him a scowl because he's clearly holding back.

Hugo lets out a heavy sigh, then mutters, "You can fuck with her in your own time, Vetrov. Let's get this over with."

Before I can take another breath, Damien moves toward me. I manage to deliver a punch to his chest as his right arm wraps around my neck, and then he moves in behind me.

Shit. The damn chokehold from hell.

He yanks me to his solid chest, his bicep cutting off my air supply. Bringing my elbow back against his ribs doesn't make him move at all, and I repeat the action as dots explode in my vision.

Damien's left arm wraps around my waist, and then I feel his breath on my ear as he whispers, "You don't belong here."

His arm tightens around my neck, and it has me grabbing hold of his forearm and bicep.

When I try to suck in a strangled breath, my body bucking against his, Damien tightens his hold on me. My vision goes black from the lack of air, and the last thing I'm aware of is Damien's body taking my full weight as I lose consciousness.

I don't know for how long I'm unconscious, but when I come to, I find myself lying on a mat and not just on the side of the room like MJ. I shake my head to rid myself of the last of the dizziness, and when I sit up, I hear Hugo chuckle, "Aww, have a soft spot for the Blood Princess?"

Did Damien move me to the mat? Why would he do that?

Knowing Damien took it easy on me makes a wave of embarrassment crash over me. Just as my sight focuses on Damien, he mutters, "Can we get back to training?"

"Lamas versus Vetrov," Grandmaster Yeoh grinds out, probably upset with MJ and me and our poor performances.

"I might as well take the day off," Paulie mumbles.

"An hour on the reflex bag," Grandmaster Yeoh instructs Paulie while Hugo and Damien face each other in the middle of the room.

Damien's standing with his back to me, and my eyes narrow on him. Anger begins to simmer in my chest because he embarrassed me in front of the whole class. Instead of sparring, he choked me to get me out of the way.

I hear groaning coming from MJ as she begins to come to, and the instant Hugo glances at her, Damien darts forward. Spinning his body, he plants the heel of his foot against Hugo's jaw.

While Hugo's still shaking his head, Damien moves in on him, delivering punches. After the sixth, Damien ends with an uppercut to Hugo's chin. This time Hugo's dazed as he staggers backward, and Damien finishes him off with a knee to his chin, knocking him out cold.

For a moment, I forget about being embarrassed and angry as I gape at Damien.

God, no one stands a chance against him.

Damien's muscles ripple as he steps away from an unconscious Hugo while grumbling, "Are we done sparring?"

Grandmaster Yeoh lets out a huff then waves an arm at the equipment.

As Damien walks toward the Wing Chun wooden dummy, he glances in my direction. Instantly the scowl on his face darkens, and then he turns his face away from me as if I'm nothing but an annoyance.

I climb to my feet, and with every step I take in Damien's direction, my anger grows.

When I reach him, I snap, "I didn't take you for a coward."

Damien shoots me a glare, and where any sane person would back away and run for cover, I have to force myself to stand my ground.

"I'm here to train. Taking it easy on me won't do me any favors," I continue as I cross my arms over my chest. Damien's jaw locks, and it makes a muscle jump in his cheek. Slowly, he turns his face to me, his eyes cold and merciless. We stare at each other, my anger and embarrassment clashing against his annoyance until I grind the words out, "Next time, treat me as an equal."

He lets out a humorless chuckle. "That's something you'll never be, *Princess*."

The egotistical sexist.

Just as I take a threatening step closer to Damien, Grandmaster Yeoh calls out, "Hemsley. Fang."

I spare Damien one last glare before I walk over to the mat Grandmaster Yeoh is waiting on. "Fight," he mutters, seemingly just as annoyed as Damien.

I take in my position with the full intention of trying to regain some of my lost pride.

DAMIEN

I should continue with my training, but I find myself turning to watch the fight. I'm not the only one. Hugo and Paulie actually step closer to the girls.

Anger still tightens Winter's features as she focuses on MJ. Winter might be beautiful, but I couldn't give two shits about offending her sensitive pride. I knew the fight between us was a no-win situation. If I hadn't taken it easy on her, she wouldn't be standing right now. I opted for the lesser evil because there's no honor in beating up someone just because I can. That's not what I'm in training for.

Besides, out in the real world, close combat is only in extreme circumstances. Like when you run out of ammo which won't happen if you're prepared at all times.

MJ throws the first punch, landing a blow to Winter's jaw. I'm surprised when there's no flash of pain on Winter's face, but instead, she goes in for the kill. She moves fast, not giving MJ a second to recover, going from throwing punches to delivering the double-knee flying kick she took Paulie out with.

MJ stumbles to the side, mumbling, "I yield."

I shake my head, wondering what MJ is even doing here.

Just then, Hugo steps forward. "How about a dance, sweetheart?"

"Fine," Grandmaster Yeoh says, not looking as irritated as he did earlier.

I cross my arms over my chest and move a little closer as Hugo starts to circle Winter. When he moves in on her, I hold my breath. The punch he delivers to the side of her head knocks her back, but she doesn't stumble like MJ did. I expect Winter to throw a couple of punches, but instead, she targets Hugo's legs, the inside of her foot connecting with the side of his knee. Winter instantly delivers another kick.

I notice the slight limp as Hugo lunges at her, his fist almost connecting with her jaw but missing.

She's using her speed against Hugo. Good girl.

Winter darts forward, swiping Hugo's feet from under him. He grabs her leg, yanking her to the floor, but before he can get a good hold of her, her legs wrap around his neck.

The corner of my mouth lifts as I watch Winter strangle Hugo with her thighs. It takes a couple of seconds before Grandmaster Yeoh calls out, "Release him. The fight's over."

Winter listens, but as she gets up, Hugo yanks her back down. Before she can catch her bearings, he begins to deliver one blow after the other.

I take a step forward but catch myself.

Winter knees Hugo in the back, and it sends him sprawling over her. As he tries to get the upper hand back, she wildly bucks her body up, and it makes him fall to the side.

I let out the breath I was holding when Winter begins to lay into Hugo, a growl rippling from her.

God, she's fierce. I underestimated her.

"The fight is over!" Grandmaster Yeoh shouts, having lost his temper with the two.

This time Winter keeps her eyes locked on Hugo as she climbs to her feet.

Hugo begins to chuckle as he spits blood onto the mat. "Not bad, Princess. Not bad at all."

Breathless from the sparring session, Winter's gaze snaps to mine, the anger back in her green eyes. The blood on her bottom lip and eyebrow make her look wild. It stirs something in my chest I've never felt before.

I nod to show her I watched, then I mutter, "Still not good enough."

"I'm ready to fight you right now," she hisses at me.

"That's enough. Both of you, go run off your anger," Grandmaster Yeoh orders. "If you fight outside of this studio, I won't train you any further."

Letting out a sigh, I strip the wrap from my hands and remove the sparring gear. I leave the studio before Winter and head toward the front doors. As soon as I step outside, I begin to jog.

Seconds later, I hear Winter's footsteps behind me. She catches up to me, but I choose to ignore her, focusing on my breaths.

When we start our sixth lap around the castle, I pick up speed. Winter increases her pace to match mine, and it makes the corner of my mouth lift.

The woman probably takes everything in life as a dare.

We keep alternating at taking the lead, and when we start our tenth lap, I give it my everything, hoping to leave her behind.

As we turn the corner of the castle and the front steps come into sight, Winter darts past me. I let out a chuckle as the distance between us grows.

Fuck, the girl is fast. At least she has that going for her. Her speed might just save her life one day.

She comes to a stop by the stairs and then rests her hands on her knees, her eyes focusing on me as she gasps for air.

I slow down to a stop in front of Winter, and it has her straightening up. Tilting my head, I lift my hand to her bottom lip, and it has her freezing. Locking eyes with her, I brush the pad of my thumb over the dried blood.

"You might have speed, but you don't have the endurance. Nice try, though." As I begin to jog away from her, I call out, "You better get some ice on your bruises."

Chapter 7

WINTER

"How's your first day going?" Cillian asks during a call.

"Okay," I mutter as I take a clean training outfit from the closet. "I had three fights."

"And?"

I lay the outfit out on my bed and walk to the bathroom. Opening the faucets so my bathwater can run, I continue, "I beat MJ Fang. The fight with Hugo Lamas was stopped, but I was winning. He's strong but slow."

Cillian chuckles, then asks, "And the third?"

"Vetrov chocked me out," I mumble.

I hear a sigh come over the line. "What did you learn from the fight against him?"

"That he's arrogant and won't fight me."

There's a moment's silence, then Cillian mutters, "Careful of Vetrov, poppet. I know I taught you to never back down, but the Vetrovs are the best."

A frown forms on my forehead. "I won't back down."

"Because you're stubborn," Cillian chastises me. "It's a weakness you need to work on."

Letting out a sigh, I mumble, "I know."

"When do you start with weapons training?"

I glance at the time. "Thirty minutes. I need to get ready, and I want to grab something to eat."

"Call me later."

"I will."

After ending the call, I close the faucets and rush through my bath routine. I can soak my muscles tonight. Once I'm dressed in a clean pair of black pants and a t-shirt, I slip on my boots. Standing up from where I was sitting on the side of the bed, I feel more confident now that I'm wearing my combat uniform. I go back into the bathroom and take a butterfly band-aid from my first aid kit. I stick it over the split above my eyebrow, and then I dab some ointment onto the cut on my lip. Having taken care of my injuries which aren't too bad, I tie my hair back in a ponytail and leave my room.

The hallway is empty as I make my way to the stairs, and I figure everyone is either busy with training or eating. I walk into the dining room and notice only three tables are occupied. Damien's sitting at the one in the far corner. I choose one close to the door, which is on the opposite side of the room.

I take a seat with my back facing the wall, so I have a clear view of the other tables. When a waiter stops by my table, I order a gourmet beef sandwich and a salad, along with a berry smoothie and a bottle of water.

I settle back in my chair, and lifting my chin, my eyes find Damien's. He's done eating and just stares at me.

He might be better than me when it comes to hand-to-hand combat, but I hope I can give him a run for his money in weaponry.

Cillian taught me to be competitive. But when it comes to Damien, something else drives me to prove to him I can stand my ground.

I'm constantly aware of the attraction I feel toward him. His piercing eyes, chiseled jaw, muscled body… and damn, the way he keeps pushing all my buttons.

An arrogant Russian God.

Only, I have zero intention of bowing to him. Ever.

As if he can read my thoughts, the corner of his mouth lifts in a dangerously sexy smirk. Not that I care. I'm sure Damien's well aware of the effect he has on women.

I watch as he rises to his feet, and then he slowly begins to stalk in my direction. When he's close, I lift my chin, my eyes locking with his.

Instead of making a remark about how I'm not good enough, his eyes keep mine prisoner until they snap away from me as he leaves the room. The moment has my heartbeat speeding up and the spit drying in my mouth. Not out of fear but something else… something far more dangerous.

Damien's the kind of man women kill for.

Shaking my head, I take a deep breath. My food arrives in time to keep me occupied, so I won't get lost in my thoughts of Damien. Or so I hope.

I think it's his intensity that has me rattled. I'm forced to notice him whenever we're in the same room, unlike the other men who can't even get a second glance from me.

As I'm finishing my meal, I hear hard footsteps, and then Carson walks into the room. His eyes skim over me before he walks to the table Damien was sitting at.

"Winter Hemsley," a voice gets my attention. I glance at the speaker, and not recognizing him, I narrow my eyes. "Adrian Vincent," he introduces himself as he takes a seat across from me.

His name registers, and I murmur, "Assassin."

He gives me a cocky smile. "At your service."

I let my gaze drift over him, taking in his black hair, his almost black eyes, and sharp features. Apprehension skitters down my spine.

Be careful of this one.

Setting my napkin down, I rise to my feet, and with one last glance at Adrian, I leave the room.

When I walk into the weapons room, I hear gunshots. Following the sound, I find the range, and for a couple of minutes, I watch Damien and Hugo firing shots at paper targets. They're both good, their bullets never missing the head and heart.

I hear movement behind me, and glancing over my shoulder, I see Paulie and MJ walking into the room with Miss Dervishi. She walks to a wide wall and presses a button, which has the wall sliding back, displaying a comprehensive selection of weapons.

Slowly, I step closer, stopping behind MJ. Hearing footsteps behind me, I have to force myself to not glance back, knowing it's Damien and Hugo. Instead, I move to the side, and crossing my arms over my chest, I take in a position that has no one standing behind me.

It's one of the first lessons Cillian taught me. Always be on guard.

Miss Dervishi glances between MJ and me. "Do you know anything about weapons?"

"A little," MJ answers, which surprises me. Her father is one of the best custodians, yet she seems grossly unprepared.

When Miss Dervishi's eyes land on me, I gesture to the selection of weapons. "Heckler & Koch P30L, my personal favorite. Glock 19, second generation. Browning Hi-power Mark 3, Heckler & Koch MP5K submachine gun, but I prefer removing the forward handguard instead of keeping the extended barrel on. It's easier to handle then. KA-BAR serrated Tanto –"

Before I can continue, Miss Dervishi nods. "At least one of you came prepared. Choose your weapon and line up by the shooting range so I can see if you know how to fire a weapon."

Without hesitating, I pick the Heckler & Koch P30L and check the clip to make sure it's loaded. An arm reaches past me to select the same weapon, and I know it's Damien without having to look. Turning away from him, I head to the shooting range, and I take the last stall, so there's no reason for someone to be behind me.

I put on ear protection, and widening my stance, I lift my arms and line the barrel up with my sight. Taking a deep breath, I slowly let it out, and then I pull the trigger. My bullet tears through the paper target's head.

Once I've emptied the clip, Miss Dervishi comes toward me. "Who trained you?"

"Cillian Byrne. My personal guard."

Her eyebrows lift, and she actually looks impressed. "You were trained by one of the best. Why are you here?"

To show my enemies, I'm someone they should fear.

"One can never be good enough," I answer instead.

With a nod, she moves onto MJ, and I reload my clip.

DAMIEN

It's been a week since classes started, and besides Winter impressing me on a daily basis, nothing has changed in my routine. There has also been no word of when the auction will take place.

When I walk into the weapons room, I'm surprised to find the assassins still here. Paulie is the last of the custodians to arrive, and then Miss. Dervishi says, "Today, you'll be paired for a game of laser tag. The last assassin standing wins. It doesn't matter if the custodian is taken out, as long as your assassin survives." Her gaze drifts over us before she continues, "Riccardo Nero and Hugo Lamas. Jet Tao and Paul Connors. Adrian Vincent and Winter Hemsley. Carson Koslov and Damien Vetrov. Miss Fang will sit this one out. Get geared up. You have five minutes."

This should be an easy win.

I walk to Carson and grin at him as we pull on our vests before grabbing our laser guns. Carson glances over the other assassins, then murmurs, "Let's show them how it's done."

When Carson begins to walk toward the door which leads outside where the abandoned building is, I flank his left side, my steps matching each of his.

Stopping by the entrance of the building, we wait for the other teams, and then Miss Dervishi says, "The music and smoke are to sharpen your instincts. There's no time limit. You don't get to leave until the last team... or man is standing. You have sixty seconds before your guns are activated. Good Luck."

Nodding, Carson disappears inside, and I follow right behind him while counting to sixty. We're instantly engulfed in darkness, unable to see anything but shadows and smoke. An intense beat fills the air, making it next to impossible to hear any movements.

We move deeper into the building, and finding stairs, I follow Carson up to a higher level where it's even darker, except for a random flash of blue light every couple of seconds.

"Three... two..." Carson counts down, and then he goes silent on one.

"Move deeper," I instruct him. "We need to go up. Let them finish each other off."

Carson nods, and turning my back to him, we stick close together. He leads me while I keep guard, making sure no one creeps up on us.

"Aww... fuck," I hear Paulie curse from somewhere in the building. "Sorry, mate."

"Idiot," Jet shouts.

"Two down," Carson mutters.

"Less for us."

We head up another flight of stairs, and this time the flashes of lights alternate between blue and red. It's a little disorientating, and I'm sure that's the goal.

We reach a couple of crates, and I gesture for Carson to take cover behind them while I take out the threats. I crouch down next to the crates, which gives me a clear view of the stairs. This way, I can pick them off as they appear.

Minutes pass in which the music fills my ears, almost matching my heartbeat.

A shadow moving grabs my attention, and I focus my sight on the spot. From the build of the person, it looks like Hugo. Before I can aim, he steps back and keeps his body hidden out of sight so I can't get a shot while he peeks around the corner.

The next minute he darts forward with Riccardo right behind him, and seconds later, all hell breaks loose as Winter and Adrian come up behind them.

Keeping my cool, I slowly rise to my feet and move to the left to get a clear shot at Riccardo.

Before I can take a shot, Riccardo's vest vibrates and lights up. It looks like Winter took the shot.

"Fuck. Thanks for nothing, Lamas," Riccardo snaps, and then he heads toward the stairs.

I duck down, but then Hugo drops his gun, and like an enraged bull, he storms Winter. He shoves his shoulder into her stomach and lifts her off the floor, slamming her into a wall.

Sore loser.

Keeping low, I move forward, knowing Hugo won't stop unless one of us intervenes. Before I reach them, Adrian slams the butt of his gun against Hugo's head, dislodging him from Winter. It gives me the perfect opportunity to shoot Adrian. I don't hesitate, and a second later, his vest lights up.

It's only then Adrian notices me. He shoves at Hugo and throws his arms wide open. "Asshole."

Hugo tackles Adrian before he can say anything else, and they begin to fight. Reaching for Winter, I grab hold of her arm and yank her away from the brawling men.

The flashing lights give us glimpses of Hugo and Adrian throwing punches. I have no intention of breaking up the fight. They can kill each other for all I care.

Winter yanks away from me, and then I hear Carson curse, "Blyad'." My eyes widen as I watch his vest light up.

I grab hold of Winter by the neck and shove her up against the wall. Our eyes lock as I growl right in her face, "What the fuck? The game's over."

Either Hugo or Adrian slams into my back, and it makes my body press hard against Winter's. A tempting grin spreads over her face as she says, "It's never over."

Chapter 8

WINTER

I get glimpses of Damien's face with every flash of light. He looks like a demon ready to rip my soul from my body.

A hot demon. I wouldn't mind if he defiled my soul right here.

His hard body presses against mine, keeping me pinned to the wall. I feel his fingers move as he flexes them around my neck.

One of the guys bumps into Damien again, and this time I feel his breath burst over my face.

The music. The lights. The adrenaline and smoke in the air. It all screws with my mind as I stare at Damien, our faces only an inch apart.

It feels as if the minutes crawl by while the fighting around us slows down to a distant blur. Damien's aftershave engulfs me, the scent mouth-wateringly good. I become highly aware of every solid inch of him, and it makes desire burst through me, more intense than anything I've felt before.

He lowers his hand from my neck, and I feel his fingers brush over my collar bone before they skim the side of my breast and down my side. He leans in, and just as his lips caress my jaw, he grabs hold of my gun and yanks it out of my hand.

For the first time in my life, I couldn't care less about losing. Not with Damien so close to me. My skin tingles for his touch, and I begin to turn my head, ready to offer my lips to him.

It's only for a split second, and then he takes a step back, severing the contact between us. Air bursts from my lungs as I realize what happened and what I almost did.

I knew Damien was dangerous, but damn, he practically had me hypnotized with lust.

Stupid, Winter!

Angry at myself, I sidestep Hugo and Adrian, who are still fighting, and rush down the stairs. When I finally step out of the building, I strip the vest from my torso and toss it aside.

Shit. I have some serious damage control to do. I can't have Damien thinking I'm attracted to him even if it's the truth.

Needing to regain control over my emotions, I head back to my personal quarters. I avoid phoning Cillian and draw myself a bath so I can relax and get my focus back on the training before going downstairs for dinner.

I strip out of my clothes, my thoughts consumed by what happened with Damien.

Damn, it was so close. How could I lose control like that?

If we were out in the real world, it would've been the perfect opportunity for him to kill me.

I step into the tub and sink down in the balmy water. Leaning my head back, I close my eyes, and then the disastrous scene begins to replay in my mind.

I clench my teeth as I remember his strong fingers wrapped around my throat. His touch burned through my skin, setting me ablaze as if a wildfire was pouring through my veins. He was so close. Too close. I felt every rippling muscle beneath his clothes.

My body flushes with heat, and it has nothing to do with the warm water I'm lying in. I could feel his hardness pressing against my abdomen. A tremble ripples through me, and I clench my thighs together, rubbing them slightly for friction.

God, I've never been so turned on in my life, and it scares me to death.

I let out a miserable sigh when my phone begins to ring, popping the lust-filled bubble I'm in.

"So much for getting my feelings under control," I mutter to myself as I climb out of the water. I wrap a towel around my body and walk to where my phone is lying on the bedside table. Seeing Cillian's name flashing on the screen draws another sight from me.

I answer the call, grumbling, "I was in the bath."

Cillian ignores my comment and asks, "How was training?"

"I got myself and my assassin killed in a game of laser tag. Today sucks. I just want to eat and sleep."

"Why did you get yourself killed?"

Because I was turned on by Damien Vetrov, and I wanted him to take me right there against the wall.

"A fight broke out, and it distracted me," I lie, but then I add, "I did shoot Carson, though."

"Good."

"I'm heading down for dinner, and then I'm calling it a night."

"Get some rest, poppet. I'll talk to you tomorrow," Cillian says before ending the call.

I drop the phone back on the bedside table then walk to my closet. Not caring about my appearance, I get dressed in a pair of gray sweatpants and a white t-shirt. I slip on my sneakers and pull a brush through my hair before I leave my room.

When I enter the dining room, Adrian rises to his feet from where he was seated at a table and begins to clap his hands. He's covered in bruises, and when he grins, it draws my attention to his busted lip.

"Winter Hemsley, the one who shot Carson Koslov. Badass," he calls out for all to hear, and it makes everyone turn their focus on me.

My face instantly flushes with heat from all the unwanted attention, and it has me snapping, "Stop. It's not like we won. You still got yourself shot."

"Have dinner with me," he says as he takes a seat again.

When I hesitate, he tilts his head and grins. "Come on. It's the least you can do after I got into a fight with Hugo to protect you."

I let out a disgruntled noise through my nose, but I sit down anyway. At least Adrian is safe, seeing as I'm not attracted to him.

"This doesn't mean we're friends," I mutter so he won't get any ideas. After all, he is an assassin in training.

Adrian's black eyes sparkle with mischief as he stares at me, then he murmurs, "Why be friends if there are so many other things we can be."

"Don't make me lose my appetite," I say as I signal a waiter closer. "I was hoping to enjoy my meal."

While I place my order, opting for a steak and baked potato with a side of vegetables, I can feel everyone's eyes still on me. I shift in my chair, and when I glance to my right, my gaze collides with Damien's. His eyes are narrowed on me, a slight frown marring his forehead.

Just having his gaze on me is enough to make my heartbeat speed up, and I quickly turn my attention back to Adrian, not wanting Damien to see how he affects me.

"I must say, you're a nice change in the boring routine," Adrian murmurs, dropping his voice low. When I just stare at him, he continues, "It's been a long two years. Hopefully, I'll be done with this place soon."

"Who will you bid on?" I ask, even though I know he won't tell me. It would be stupid of him.

He shakes his head and then surprises me by saying, "No one. I prefer to work alone. I'm sticking around for my own contract and to see who's pairing up."

I nod, and the conversation stops as a waiter brings my cranberry juice. I take a sip and set the glass down to the side, so I don't accidentally knock it over.

Feeling eyes on me again, I glance at Damien, and instantly his intense gaze clashes with mine. It sends a lightning streak through my body.

"What's the deal with you and Vetrov?" Adrian asks, drawing my attention back to him.

I shrug and lean back in my chair, trying to look relaxed. "Nothing. He finds me annoying, and I think he's arrogant."

Adrian lets out a chuckle as if he doesn't believe me. "Damien doesn't waste his time with anyone unless there's something to gain. I saw the two of you snuggling up while I was kicking Hugo's ass."

My eyes narrow on Adrian as I reach for my glass, taking a slow sip of my juice. Once I set it down again, I mutter, "He was disarming me. That's all it was."

Another chuckle bursts over Adrian's lips. "If you say so."

We stare at each other, and then his eyes drop to the scar on my neck. "Why are you training as a custodian?"

"Why not?" I counter his question.

His lips curve up. "I love a woman with secrets." Just as I'm about to get uncomfortable, Adrian snaps his fingers in the air. "We should get a drink and toast the fact that you shot Koslov." He orders two glasses of champagne, then reverts to looking at me. "No one's been able to do that before."

"Lucky me," I mumble. I'm proud of myself, but I'm not about to be arrogant about it.

A server brings the champagne, and Adrian takes a glass. He waits for me to pick mine up, and then he lifts his glass to mine. "Here's to you getting past Vetrov's defenses."

It sounds like his words carry a double meaning, and not ready to think about what it might mean, I down half my champagne.

DAMIEN

Watching Adrian and Winter toast their so-called win, my jaw clenches.

"You keep looking at her," Carson calls me out. "Has she gotten under your skin, and that's why I got shot?"

My eyes snap to his. "The game was over."

Carson glances at Winter. "Is it really over?"

A frown forms on my forehead, and not wanting Carson to doubt me, I mutter, "My loyalty lies with you."

He pours us each a shot of vodka, and after we've downed it, he says, "You should fuck her and get her out of your system."

Before today, I would've been able to tell Carson to go to hell, but after seeing the desire in Winter's eyes…

I shake my head at Carson, and needing to change the subject, I ask, "Have you heard anything about the auction?"

"Nothing." He rubs a hand over his day-old stubble. "Everyone's growing impatient."

I nod as my eyes find Winter again, and I watch as she takes a bite of her steak.

At first, the fear in her eyes was a turn-on. But after seeing the lust burning in her gaze, it triggered something else in me. Something primal. For the first time in my life, I want to claim a woman. Not for one night. Not for a quick release. I want to own her in every way and bend her to my will. I want to make the Blood Princess kneel before me.

"That's better," Carson says, ripping my attention away from Winter. "Now it looks like you want to kill her."

I suck in a breath of air and pour myself another drink, feeling jarred by the strong desire I feel toward Winter.

This is not good. I need to put an end to it. Maybe I should fuck her and get it over with, so my focus can be on keeping Carson alive.

Movement catches my eye, and I watch as Vince Blanco gets up from his table. When Hugo also gets up, and they leave the dining room together, a frown forms on my face. "See what I see?"

"Yeah. Blanco will probably bid on Lamas," Carson gives voice to my thoughts.

"They'll get each other killed. They're both hotheaded," I mutter.

I enjoy another two drinks with Carson, and when I get up, I notice Winter leaving the room. Glancing back at the table she shared with Adrian, I see she hasn't finished her meal, and I wonder if Adrian pissed her off.

Probably. He pisses me off just by breathing.

"See you tomorrow," I murmur to Carson, and then I leave.

Before I reach the doors, Lucian Cotroni calls out, "Vetrov, a moment." I stop by his table and raise an eyebrow at him, which has him asking, "Is Carson open for business?"

Lucian Cotroni will take over from his father, who's the head of the Mafia. You don't ignore them when they speak. I shrug, "You'll have to ask him yourself."

Lucian holds my gaze as he nods. "I'll do just that."

Nodding at him, I head toward the door, ready to call it a night. I take the stairs up and walk to my door. As I push it open, a muffled cry grabs my attention. Frowning, I slowly walk down the hallway. I'm just about to pass by Winter's room when something slams against her door.

Fuck.

For a moment, I hesitate, but then I grab hold of the doorknob and shove the door open. I'm met with Hugo pinning Winter's arms down on the floor while Vince straddles her.

Anger floods me at the sight, and it has me growling, "Am I late for the party?"

Both men look in my direction, and then Hugo lets go of Winter. Rising to his feet, he says, "This doesn't concern you, Vetrov. Fuck off."

Stepping into the room, I shut the door behind me. "Two men against one woman? I think I'll stay and even the odds."

My family lives by a code. We don't kill for pleasure. We don't rape. We don't prey on the weak. Anything else is fair game.

"Suit yourself," Hugo growls, and then he storms me. I move to my left and deliver a kick right into his gut. It sends him staggering backward, and it has Vince climbing to his feet. Hugo regains his balance and storms me again. This time I take the impact of his body. Using his shoulders to brace myself, I bring my knee repeatedly up, delivering blow after blow to his chin and nose until he drops backward.

My eyes snap to Vince. It looks like he's about to piss himself. Like I said, he's no fighter.

"You're choosing the wrong side of this war," Vince snarls at me.

I just stare at him until he steps over Hugo, trying to get to the door.

Winter struggles to sit up, and she looks out of it.

"What did you do to her?" I growl.

Vince gives Winter a deadly glare. "I just had her drugged. Unfortunately, I can't kill her. Yet."

Before I can reign in my temper, my arm shoots out, and I deliver a crushing blow to Vince's nose. Blood spurts from him like a fountain as he staggers back.

Shock registers on his face, and then he growls, "You're a dead man walking, Vetrov." Like the coward he is, he runs from the room, leaving Hugo behind.

I walk to Winter, where she's still trying to sit up while wiping blood from her lip.

Crouching by her, I say, "Next time, lock your door."

"I can't feel... anything," she mumbles.

I take hold of her chin and lift her face to mine. The first thing I notice is the glassy look in her eyes. Whatever drug Blanco gave her must be taking effect.

She begins to tip sideways, and I catch her by her shoulders. "You okay?"

Winter shakes her head, then mumbles, "Dizzy and numb... weird."

"Blyad'," I mutter. I can't just leave her alone tonight. She'll be vulnerable to attacks. God only knows what Vince and Hugo were planning on doing to her.

Chapter 9

WINTER

Mother of saints, I'm exhausted. It feels like I haven't slept in weeks.

Damien's face appears in front of me, and then darkness tints the edges of my vision. I feel his arm slide around my back and another under my knees, and then my world tilts as he lifts me from the floor.

The side of my head falls to his shoulder, and for a moment, I have a clear view of his neck and jaw, both looking kissable. It's only for a couple of seconds, though, and then my vision blurs again.

Damien begins to walk, every forceful step he takes vibrating through my body.

Crap, where is he taking me?

I try to lift my hand, and my knuckles brush against his chest before my arm goes numb again. "Where?" I manage to mumble.

"Shhh." It sounds more like a threatening hiss than a sound of comfort, and it makes the hair on my body rise.

My mind feels clouded as if I can't wake up. As if I'm stuck between reality and a nightmare. All I remember from earlier was not feeling well, and when I got to my room, Vince and Hugo were there waiting for me. I managed to fight them off, but as the drug took more of an effect on my body, they overpowered me. If Damien didn't show up, I'd probably be dead by now.

Damien… He can kill me, and there's nothing I can do to defend myself.

The thought sobers me a little, enough to lift my head from Damien's shoulder as he walks into another room. He kicks the door shut behind us, the sound echoing through my dazed mind.

Damien's arms are strong beneath me, taking my full weight as if I'm as light as a feather, even though it feels as if I weigh a ton and gravity is fighting to drag me back down to the ground.

The moment he walks into a bedroom, fear trickles down my spine.

He wouldn't.

Would he?

No. The Vetrovs have honor. He wouldn't rape me.

When he lies me down on the bed, and our eyes meet, there's nothing I can do to hide the fear I feel. The last time I was this vulnerable was the day I lost my mother and almost lost my own life.

I never thought I'd feel that way again. Hopeless. Lost. Terrified. But here I am, at the mercy of Damien Vetrov.

I try to push against the mattress to get myself up into a sitting position, but whatever drug Vince gave me makes my bones heavy and my muscles numb.

How did he manage to drug me? Did he pay one of the waiters to spike my drink?

Lying paralyzed on Damien's bed, my eyes lock on his. God, he looks even more intense and dangerous now that I'm unable to protect myself.

Damien braces his hands on either side of my head, and I'm instantly engulfed in the scent of his aftershave and heat coming from his body.

My heartbeat speeds up, and my breathing falters. "Don't," I manage to mumble.

His eyes hold mine captive as he leans a little forward and then his lips part. "I don't like my women weak. Sleep."

I search his face for any sign that he's lying to me, but only find truth. There's zero desire in his eyes. If anything, he looks angry.

I never thought I'd be relieved to see him annoyed with me. The fear retreats a little but then a new one forms. I'm going to owe Damien for this. I'm in his debt, and that's dangerous.

The cloud in my mind thickens, making me feel even more powerless. My eyes stay glued to Damien's as he straightens up. It looks like he's going to leave, and needing to get the words out, I mumble, "Thank…" I suck in a breath, and I have to really focus to finish, "…you."

His gaze narrows on me, and for a moment, he looks indecisive, but then he murmurs, "Sleep, Winter. For tonight you're safe."

Even though I know I can believe his words, I still fight the darkness skirting around the edges of my mind.

Damien disappears out of my line of sight, and I try to turn my head but unable to move, I can only listen as he opens a closet. I hear the fabric of his clothes rustle, and minutes later, he appears as he walks into the bathroom. He's only wearing black sweatpants. His muscles ripple beneath his tanned skin as he takes hold of his toothbrush.

Watching him brush his teeth and wash his face calms me. All I can do is stare at him while my breaths grow rhythmic. I take in every curve of muscle, every vein snaking up his arm. When he walks back to me, I drink in the wide expanse of his chest, his abs, and the carved lines of his hips as they dip under his low-hanging sweatpants.

My emotions scatter, desire mixing with the vulnerability I feel, and it makes something new stir in my chest.

Cillian taught me to fight, to always be strong, but lying on Damien's bed, I wonder what it would be like to be dominated by him. To have him take over the reins in my life. To be in control of me.

Would I find peace and safety, or would I be destroyed?

What's the use of thinking about it. I probably won't remember any of this tomorrow.

Damien turns off the lights, and I hear as he moves through the room. I feel the mattress dip as he lies down, and it makes my heart rate spike.

Never in my wildest dreams did I think I'd share a bed with a Vetrov. Now there's one lying mere inches from me.

The stories Cillian told me about Demitri made the Vetrovs seem merciless and cold. Monsters who wouldn't hesitate to kill. After all, Demitri played a significant role in eliminating an Albanian group.

Up until tonight, I believed every word, but now I've seen a soft side to Damien. He could've ignored my predicament. He could've left me lying in my room, vulnerable to another attack.

But he didn't.

He brought me to his room, and now he's lying beside me… guarding me.

Who is the real Damien Vetrov?

This man who's protecting me, or will he turn out to be a legendary killer like his brother?

With the thoughts mulling in my head, my eyes drift shut. The last thing I'm aware of before the drug drags me under a wave of numbing darkness is the intensity coming from Damien's presence beside me.

DAMIEN

For a moment, I regret helping Winter, but then I remember the scene I walked in on. Hugo holding her down while Vince was on top of her.

It makes my anger return, not because they were probably going to rape her, but because they dared to touch her. A possessive side I never knew I had flared to life, making me see red. It pushed me forward to destroy… to kill… all for her.

By the grace of God, I didn't kill them. It would've ruined everything I worked so hard for.

Turning my head, I stare at Winter's profile. It looks like she's fallen asleep. Good. Seeing the fear in her eyes made the blood rush through my veins. It was intoxicating.

Having her at my mercy makes desire burn in me, and it makes me want to claim her for myself.

But I don't want her this way. I want her to fight back. I want to see the spark in her eyes. I want her lips to part as I thrust into her. I want to hear her moans and screams as I fuck her, branding her with my cock.

Like any other predator, I enjoy the thrill of the hunt, and right now, she's nothing more than a wounded deer.

My gaze drifts down to her breasts, and I watch as they rise and fall with every slow breath she takes.

Turning onto my side, I reach a hand out to her neck and let my fingers brush over her throat. "There's a price to pay for my protection, Princess," I whisper. I let my fingers trail down her chest, passing between the curves of her breasts and down to her hip. Pulling her closer, I push my other arm under her head and turn her body into mine. I take in the feel of holding her, and then, I murmur, "The only payment I'll accept is your body, heart, and soul."

Never before in my life have I wanted a woman the way I want Winter Hemsley. I want to own her fiery temper. I want to possess her wild spirit. I want to dominate her body, forcing her to submit to me… and only me.

A growl escapes my throat as my arms tighten around her. The wild emotions almost overwhelm me, but I yank back and push her away from me. Winter rolls limply onto her back as my breath explodes from me.

Blyad'.

I can't give in to my desires. They'll derail everything I've worked for.

My loyalty belongs to Carson, which means there's no place in my life for a woman.

With every muscle in my body wound tight, I keep staring at Winter. This night. It's all I'm giving myself. I'll drink in her beauty and the soft sound of her breaths.

Knowing better, I still lift my hand again and reach for her.

Just tonight. Then I'll ban all thoughts of her from my mind. I'll get my shit together and focus on Carson.

Wrapping my hand around the side of her waist, I pull Winter back to me. Knowing this is all I'll allow myself to have, I lean into her until I can feel her breaths warming my lips. I take a deep breath, filling my lungs with her soft scent.

As I wrap my arms around her, I close my eyes and try to memorize the feel of her body pressing against mine.

I lie awake through the night, and with every hour I get to hold Winter, my emotions deepen, opening up a bottomless cavern inside my chest.

By the time the sun begins to rise, and Winter's lashes flutter open, I feel murderous.

Her green irises focus on my face, and then her eyes widen with shock. Before she can start fighting me, I pull away from her and get up. I stalk to my closet and take a rashguard shirt and pair of shorts from it.

"What am I doing here?" Winter tries to demand with a sleepy voice. I hear her move off the bed. "God, my head," she mumbles.

Turning to face her, the words leave me in a low grumble, "You were drugged by Blanco. He and Lamas had you pinned down in your room. I brought you here so you'd be safe while the drug worked out of your system." My eyes lock on her wide ones, and I watch as her shock grows. "Which means you owe me, Princess."

Her tongue darts out over her dry lips, wetting them in a nervous action. "How much?"

I let out a dark chuckle as I drop the clean clothes on the bed. Shaking my head at her, I murmur, "I don't want your money."

Winter begins to move slowly toward the door, and it makes the corner of my mouth lift slightly.

"What do you want?" she asks, sounding a little breathless.

My eyes lock with hers. "I'll let you know when I'm ready to claim my payment."

I watch as her features tighten with worry. Her owing me puts me in a position of power, and she doesn't like it one bit.

"Leave." The single word is clipped before I walk into the bathroom so I can shower.

For a moment longer, I feel Winter's eyes on me, and when I look to where she was standing, she's gone.

Chapter 10

WINTER

I rush to my room, and shutting the door behind me, I make sure to lock it. When I turn around, I take in the overturned furniture and the blood on the floor.

What the hell happened last night?

I try to search my memory, but the last I remember was heading downstairs for dinner.

Damien said Vince drugged me, that he and Hugo attacked me. Damien intervened and took to me to his room?

I don't remember any of it, and now I'm in his debt. God.

Waking up in Damien's bed with his face so close to mine... the memory makes heat flood my body. When he climbed out of bed, and I got a look at his bare chest and the low-hanging sweatpants, I almost pinched myself to make sure I wasn't dreaming.

No, Winter. Focus.

The more I try to make sense of what happened, the more my head begins to pound with a headache. It feels like I have the hangover from hell.

Walking to my bathroom, I open the faucets in the shower and brush my teeth while I let the water run. When I pull the t-shirt over my head, I glance down at the bruises and hand imprints on my torso. Lifting my head, I stare at the cut on my bottom lip and the purple swelling under my left eye.

My body begins to tremble when I think of how close I came to being raped... killed.

Stripping out of my sweatpants and underwear, I step under the warm spray, and I let the drops pelt my skin to life. My legs shake from having to keep myself standing, and I place a hand against the tiled wall.

My stomach rolls and I quickly press my other hand to it as a wave of nausea hits.

God, I feel like shit.

Taking deep breaths, I wait for my stomach to settle, and then I wash every inch of my body. When I step out of the shower, I dry myself without looking at the bruises. On weak legs, I walk to the closet, and taking out clean clothes for training, I get dressed while anger simmers in my chest.

I'd love nothing more than to crawl into bed and to sleep the hangover away, but I can't. I need to show Vince he didn't get to me. I need to be stronger than ever right now.

After pulling a brush through my damp hair, I leave it to air dry as I take deep breaths in an attempt to steel myself for the day ahead. It's not going to be easy, but I have to get through it with my head held high.

I ignore the mess in the living room, hoping the staff will have it cleaned before I return. As I leave my quarters, I glance up and down the hallway, my body on guard for a sudden attack. I feel edgy as I make my way to the stairs, and I slowly descend them.

When I walk into the dining room, I don't look at the other patrons but head to the table in the corner. I sit with my back to the wall, and when a waiter comes, I give him a wary look.

Can I trust anything I eat and drink here?

"Cranberry juice," I mutter. "In a sealed bottle." When he nods, I continue, "Bacon, two eggs, and toast."

I need the greasy breakfast to help my stomach settle, or I'll be puking at training.

Movement catches my eye, and my gaze snaps from the waiter to Adrian as he takes a seat at my table.

"I didn't invite you to sit with me," I say.

Ignoring my words, he places his own order, then his eyes meet mine. "I heard what happened last night. I thought you'd want to talk business."

"Business?"

"Gun for hire," he murmurs.

"You can't kill Blanco while he's on St. Monarch's property, so I have no use for you."

Adrian stares at me, long and hard, and then the corner of his mouth tips up. "For the right amount, I'm willing to take the risk."

It feels as if his words carry a double meaning, and it makes my heart rate spike.

Would Adrian really kill on the grounds and risk being banned?

"Move," Damien suddenly growls next to the table.

Both Adrian and my heads snap up. Adrian locks gazes with Damien, and after a couple of seconds, he gets up, muttering, "Playing the hero is damaging your reputation. Careful, Vetrov."

I watch as the two men stare at each other, and then Adrian leaves. Damien takes the vacated chair and pins me with a dark glare that I feel penetrating through the feeble barrier I've manage to put up after last night.

After waking in his bed, it's harder to ignore the fluttering in my stomach and the need tightening my abdomen whenever he's near.

"Don't get yourself killed before settling your debt with me."

I narrow my eyes on him. "Are you going to remind me that I owe you every chance you get?"

"If you continue to place yourself in danger… yes," he grumbles.

A frown begins to form on my forehead. "Give me an amount, and I'll settle the debt, then you won't have to worry."

The corner of his mouth lifts, making him look predatory as his eyes darken. It causes a fluttering in my stomach, a mixture of nerves and attraction.

"I don't like repeating myself," he murmurs, his voice deep.

Luckily a server brings my order, and I get to keep myself busy with opening the bottle of juice.

"You had dinner with Adrian when you were drugged," Damien breaks the silence, and then he rises to his feet. "That bit of information is free."

I watch as he walks away, confused why he'd tell me that. Information is power in our world. Still, he told me.

My eyes leave Damien's broad back and snap to where Adrian is sitting. For the right price, he's willing to break the rules of the academy. Is he on Vince's payroll?

My gaze darts to another table where Hugo is seated. His nose is crooked, and half his face is swollen with bruises.

Damien did that.

For me.

Only when I see the damage Damien did to Hugo's face do I realize there are no bruises on Damien. Vince walks in, and he, too, looks like he ran face first into a wall.

As Vince takes a seat, his eyes meet mine. I let my mouth curve up in a sneer to show him I'm not rattled by what he did.

Bastard.

DAMIEN

Last night she took a beating, and she must have a hangover from the drug, but still, there she sits. I watch the daring smile curve around her lips as she faces off with

Vince, and it makes the now familiar feeling stir in my chest.

Respect.

Winter Hemsley doesn't cower before her enemies. She's braver than most men I know. And it only makes me want her more.

Christ, I want to own that wild spirit of hers.

"I heard what happened," Carson says as he takes a seat, a dark frown marring his forehead. "Why did you intervene?"

"She owes me now," I mutter.

Carson's eyes lock on mine. "I wasn't aware you were conducting business on the grounds."

"I'm not, but having the Hemsleys in my debt was worth it."

Carson nods, then he turns his gaze to Winter. "Did you at least fuck her out of your system?"

No, I held her all fucking night like she was mine.

"Stop worrying about it. I won't fuck up as your custodian," I assure him.

Carson brings his eyes back to me. "You better not. The auction is tomorrow night at eight."

What?

"When did you hear this?" I ask.

"If you weren't so absorbed with the Blood Princess, you would've seen the invite. It's probably in your quarters."

I get up so fast it sends the chair toppling back, and without another word, I leave the dining room. When I shove my door open, I spot the black envelope. Picking it up, exhilaration begins to slither down my spine.

I open the envelope, and my eyes scan over the gold embroidered words. I have one hour left to RSVP. Walking to my bedroom, I pick up my phone and text the code provided to the number.

Instantly my phone beeps, and the message appears.

RESERVED.

It's happening. I'm finally done with this place. In two days, I'll leave with Carson, and we'll join Demitri and Alexei.

Fucking finally.

Knowing everything I've worked so hard for is within my grasp, I leave my quarters and walk to the sparring studios. I have to be in my best shape for tomorrow night.

When I walk into the studio where most of the training equipment is held, Paulie grins at me. "You're going to miss me."

I shake my head. "Not a chance in hell."

I strap on a pair of shin guards and the rest of my gear, then make my way over to a punching bag so I can warm up. I spend thirty minutes punching the shit out of the bag before I grab a jumping rope.

"Fuck off," I hear Winter growl.

Glancing over my shoulder, I watch as she straps on her gear with Hugo standing over her.

"One last fight," he grumbles.

Winter's head snaps up, and her features are tight with anger. "I said fuck off, Lamos. I don't waste my time on cowards."

It looks like they're a second away from tearing into each other when Grandmaster Yeoh walks into the studio. "Miss Hemsley, you're with me."

She gives Hugo a last dark glare before she shoves past him to join Grandmaster Yeoh.

I begin with my rope jumping session while watching Winter train. She doesn't miss a beat even though she must feel like shit after last night.

Tearing my eyes away from her, I focus on my own training until my sweat soaks my clothes.

Tomorrow I'm done with this place.

I'll become Carson's custodian.

He'll get his first contract, and I'll make sure he's safe while he takes out the target.

I keep repeating the words as I move from doing situps to the weight bench.

After tomorrow Winter will no longer be a distraction.

Chapter 11

WINTER

All training has been canceled for the day, and I thought I'd be able to sleep in late, but I'm woken by the incessant ringing of my phone.

Squinting at the screen, I see Cillian's name flashing and grumble, "What? I'm sleeping."

"Get up and dressed. Your father and brother are here, and I'm bringing them to the academy in thirty minutes."

"What?" I gasp as I shoot upright in the bed. "They're here? Why?"

"The auction."

Oh, right.

"Still, they should be on the island," I argue.

"They get to see you for a day, poppet. Get ready." Cillian ends the call, and I drop the phone back on the bedside table.

Honestly, I've missed them, and I can do with some family time.

I get up and walk to the bathroom. Looking in the mirror, my eyes drift over the bruises.

I'll tell them it was training. They don't need to know Vince attacked me.

I rush through my morning routine, and even though there's no training, I still put on a combat outfit. I've just pulled a brush through my hair when there's a knock at my door.

Instantly excitement bursts in my chest, and I run for the door. I yank it open, and then I let out a happy shriek as I throw my arms around Dad's neck. "I missed you."

Dad chuckles as he hugs me back, and when he lets go of me, I reach for Sean.

I hug Cillian as well and let them into the room. Shutting the door, I turn to smile at my family. "This is a nice surprise, but you should've stayed on the island."

"And miss the chance of seeing you?" Dad clicks his tongue. "Never." His eyes drift over my face, and then he shakes his head. "Look at you."

I shrug his concern away. "It's nothing. You should see what the other guy looks like."

My comment draws a grin from Cillian, then he brags, "She shot Carson Koslov in a game of laser tag."

Dad's eyebrows rise as pride settles on his face. "I always knew you had it in you. A born fighter."

We take a seat in the living room, and I turn my attention to my brother. "Have you been keeping out of trouble?"

"I walked in on him shagging Anja," Dad grumbles, sounding disgruntled. Anja's one of the guards' daughters who comes to visit twice a year.

My eyes widen on my brother, and I gasp at him, "Sean!"

Sean rolls his eyes and shakes his head. "Can we not talk about it."

"He's young and horny," Cillian stands up for Sean. "Let the boy have some fun."

"I just don't want to know about it or see it," Dad mutters, then he turns his attention back to me. "Tell me about training. Have you learned anything new?"

I bring my family up to date with everything that's happened since I last saw them, sans anything Damien related and the incident with Vince and Hugo.

"Order breakfast and feed your old man," Dad says, pride shining from his eyes.

I call the kitchen and place our orders.

Dad clears his throat then says, "I spoke with Madame Keller about you learning some African languages."

I nod. "That's a good idea. I'll be able to communicate and understand the tribes whenever we're there to take receipt of a shipment."

"She said she'll email you the new schedule," Dad says.

After our breakfast arrives, I spend the rest of the morning and afternoon visiting with my family before they have to leave.

As I show them to the door, Dad asks, "Will you wear the silver dress tonight?"

I shake my head. "It will be a waste. As an attendee of the academy, I can only watch from a balcony."

Dad nods. "It's a pity. I would've liked to see you in it."

A frown forms on my face. "You're coming?"

"Yes, I want to see what's on the table tonight."

"Be careful," I whisper as I lean in to hug him.

As Dad and Sean step out of the room, Cillian gives my arms a squeeze. "Don't worry, poppet. I'll keep them safe."

My eyes meet his. "Please."

I watch them walk down the hallway and wave a last time before they disappear down the stairs.

I shut the door again and then walk to my closet to change into a fresh pair of cargo pants and a t-shirt for the night. Wanting to watch as everyone arrives, I quickly tie my hair back before I leave the room. Stopping at the top of the stairs, I rest my forearms on the banister. I have a clear view of the front doors, and my attention is glued to the people as they step inside St. Monarch's.

Lucian Cotroni catches my eye as he walks toward the front doors, and then I see why. His father, Luca, comes in, and they hug before they stand to the side so crates can be carried in. They're probably auctioning weapons tonight.

One after the other families arrive, each with whatever they're putting up for sale.

When Sonia Terrero, the Queen of Terror, comes in with two girls covered in coats with hoodies, I pull a disgusted face.

Delicious aftershave grabs my attention, and then Damien comes to stand next to me. "Selling diamonds tonight?" he asks.

I straighten up and let my eyes drift over the black three-piece suit he's wearing. It fits his body like a glove.

Damn, he looks hot.

When I take too long to answer because I'm practically drooling over him, he says, "I saw your family earlier."

"Oh." Shaking my head, I have to tear my eyes away from him. "No, we don't have anything on auction."

We watch as more people arrive, and then Damien turns his head, and his eyes lock on mine with an intense stare. A long moment pass and then he leans into me, and with his mouth brushing over my jaw, he murmurs, "It was nice meeting you, Princess. Try not to get yourself killed."

The brief contact and words stun me while making me tremble, and too late, I realize Damien's saying goodbye. I stare after him as he takes the stairs down, and unable to stop myself, I call out, "What about the debt?"

In response to my question, he only smirks at me before he disappears under the landing I'm standing on.

Then it hits. Damien won't be here tomorrow, and a sudden pang of loss makes my heart constrict.

DAMIEN

The night feels endlessly long, but at least all the goods have been auctioned off.

Madame Keller stands behind a podium, taking bids. When the two sex slaves are escorted onto the stage, I get up to leave the hall. Unable to stop myself, I glance up to the balcony where Winter is seated with her personal guard. My gaze locks on her as I walk to the door and when she glances down at me, the corner of my mouth lifts.

I head to the backstage entrance where I'll be able to watch the bidding for the assassins, and then it will be the custodians' turn.

Finding Carson as he watches the auction from the side of the stage, I ask, "Nervous?"

"Not at all," he murmurs. "I just hope it's a good contract."

"Yeah, I'm excited to start working."

"Next up for bidding are the assassins," Madame Keller announces. "Adrian Vincent. Son of the late Bruno Vincent. Achievements; one-point-five-kilometer shot, forty-seven kills during a training session."

She waits for Adrian to take his place on stage, then continues, "Jet Tao. First assassin in his family. Achievements; nine hundred meter shot, eighteen kills during a training session."

After Jet goes to stand next to Adrian, Madame Keller introduces the next assassin, "Riccardo Nero. Second generation assassin and son of Sergio Nero. Achievements; One-point-six-kilometer shot, thirty-eight kills during a training session."

I pat Carson on the back when he moves forward just as Madame Keller says, "Carson Koslov. Third generation assassin. Son of the late Marko Koslov and younger brother of Alexei Koslov. Achievements; two-point-one-kilometer shot, breaking Alexei Koslov's record of two kilometers. One hundred and three kills during a training session breaking Alexei Koslov's record of ninety-three kills."

I hear murmurs from the crowd as Carson steps out onto the stage. My eyes are locked on him as Madame Keller says, "Please enter your bids."

I find myself holding my breath as everyone enters their chosen amounts.

When Madame Keller clears her throat, I lift my chin, and my focus shifts to her.

"Adrian Vincent is contracted for nine million euros."

She won't say who won the bid. Not when it comes to the assassins, but Adrian definitely got a high-value target for that amount.

"Jet Tao is contracted for five hundred euros."

I grimace at the low amount.

"Riccardo Nero is contracted for four million euros."

I suck in a deep breath of air and hold it.

"Carson Koslov is contracted for twelve million euros."

Instantly a smile splits over my face. As Carson comes off the stage, I pull him into a brotherly hug. "Congratulations."

He pulls free from me. "I better get down there before I miss bidding on you."

With a grin, I watch him jog away, and then I turn my attention back to the stage.

"Next up for bidding are the custodians," Madame Keller announces. "Hugo Lamas. Second generation custodian. Son of Nicco Lamas. Achievements; eight seconds reaction time. Nine-second knockout of Paul Connors. Five-second knockout of MJ Fang. One thousand, six hundred and seventeen targets out of two thousand."

Hugo walks out onto the stage, his face still covered in bruises from the beating I gave him.

Madame Keller continues, "Paul Conners. Third generation custodian. Son of Charlie Conners. Achievements; ten seconds reaction time. Thirteen-second knock-out of Hugo Lamas. One thousand, six hundred and eighty-nine targets out of two thousand."

Paulie gives me a grin as he walks out onto the stage, and then it's my turn as Madame Keller introduces me,

"Damien Vetrov. Third generation custodian. Son of the late Sacha Vetrov. Younger brother of Demitri Vetrov. Achievements; broken all pre-existing records set by Demitri Vetrov. Three seconds reaction time. Two seconds knock-out of Paul Conners. Four seconds knock-out of Hugo Lamas. One thousand, nine hundred and seventy-seven targets out of two thousand."

I follow after Hugo and Paulie and take my place on the stage. My eyes instantly find Carson as he drops down in a chair.

"Please enter your bids," Madame Keller instructs.

I watch as Carson types in an amount. It better be double what Alexei paid for my brother.

The thought almost makes me smile, but I catch myself in time.

Again Madame Keller clears her throat, and slowly I take a deep breath.

"Hugo Lamas is contracted to Sonia Terrero for three million euros."

Probably to guard her daughter, which means he'll be stuck at the academy until she graduates.

"Paul Connors is contracted to Riccardo Nero for three million euros."

Good for you, Paulie.

"Damien Vetrov is contracted to Patrick Hemsley for twenty-five million euros."

Pins and needles spread over my whole body. "What?" I snap as my gaze darts between Carson and Madame Keller. A chorus of surprised murmurs floods the hall.

"The contracts are effective for twelve months," Madame Keller bites the words out, clearly angered at my reaction.

Blyad'.

My eyes snap back to Carson, and I watch as he rises to his feet, the same shock I feel etched deep on his face.

Pissed off, I stalk off the stage, and when I burst through the backstage door, Carson comes jogging toward me. "It's just twelve months. It's a good contract. I'll buy you out afterward."

"What the fuck just happened?" I spit.

"Hemsley outbid me. I put in fifteen million. No one has ever bid higher than eleven million. It was a safe bet."

Holy fuck. This was not the plan.

Lifting a hand, I rub a palm over my jaw while shaking my head. "Blyad'," I curse again. "This was not the plan." My eyes lock with Carson's. "You have no one to protect you."

"I'll join Alexei," he tries to reassure me of his safety.

Then it really sinks in, and anger explodes behind my eyes. When I push past him so I can face off with Patrick Hemsley, Carson grabs hold of my arm. "The contract is binding, Damien. Don't do something stupid. The payment has already been made, and you have to honor it."

I rip my arm free from Carson's hold and stalk to the hall. When I step inside, my eyes scan over the bidders, and then they lock on Patrick, where the other bidders are taking turns to shake his hand.

Then his body jerks, and a thin stream of blood runs down his temple before he drops to his knees. It happens so fast, it takes a moment to register that Patrick Hemsley was just assassinated. On St. Monarch's grounds.

Training takes over, and I run for Sean Hemsley, who's staring in horror at his dead father. I jump over a chair, and I don't even make it halfway before the son's body flies forward and screams erupt from the attendees.

Five seconds and I lost two charges.

I've failed within seconds of being contracted.

Winter.

My eyes dart over the attendees' section, but it's chaos as everyone either ducks or tries to make a run for it. Not seeing Winter, I can only hope she's not in the hall.

I run for the side door, and a bullet narrowly misses me, sending icy chills down my spine.

Fuck, I'm a target as well.

It has to be Adrian. Now I understand why he was contracted for such a high amount.

The instant I rush out of the door, I catch a glimpse of red hair disappearing out the front door. I dart forward and shove people out of my way.

Finally, I lay eyes on her, where she's practically being carried away from the academy by her personal guard, who's struggling to keep ahold of her. Relief pours through me at the sight of her.

"Stop, Winter!" her guard snaps, his voice tense.

I take the stairs down and run toward them. Catching up to them as they reach an armored jeep, I shout, "Give me the keys."

The personal guard only spares me a glance before he tosses them to me, and then he bundles Winter into the backseat where he joins her.

My first night on the fucking job, and I don't even have a weapon.

The thought makes another burst of anger explode in me, and a string of Russian curses escape me as I slide behind the steering wheel. "Where are the weapons?" I bark as I start the engine.

"Under the seat," the guard growls at me as he begins to pull weapons out from under the back seat. He throws two on the passenger seat as I floor the peddle, making the wheels squeal as we pull away.

A bullet slams into the back window but bounces off, and it has Winter letting out a cry. It's the first sound she's made.

I keep my eyes on the driveway as I speed toward the gates, and they open just in time for me to steer the jeep off the campus.

Slamming my palm against the steering wheel, I shout, "Blyad'!"

In one night, all my carefully laid plans have gone up in smoke, and I lost two charges.

Winter lost her father and brother.

Christ.

"Phone," I snap at the guard.

He tosses his cellphone onto my lap, and I dial my brother's number while keeping one eye on the road ahead.

"Vertov," Demitri barks over the line.

"It's Damien," I mutter.

I hear him sigh with relief. "What the fuck is going on at the academy?"

"Patrick Hemsley contracted me. He and the son were assassinated within minutes. I think it's Adrian Vincent. I don't know where Carson is. It was a mess."

"Carson got out. He called Alexei. Where's the third Hemsley?"

"I have her," I breathe, and then relief bleeds into my veins.

I have Winter.

"What do you need?" my brother asks.

"Everything," I grind the word out. "I need everything. Passports. A plane. A fucking safe house. Weapons."

"Damien!" Demitri snaps. "Take a breath. You need to be calm, or you'll get her killed. If that happens…"

He doesn't have to finish the sentence. If Winter dies on my watch, it will be the end of my career as a custodian.

Chapter 12

WINTER

No.

No.

No.

"Winter." Cillian takes hold of my chin and lifts my face to his. "Oh, poppet. I'm so sorry."

No.

"You can reach me on this number. I'll get a burner as soon as it's safe to stop. I'll text you the new number," Damien says to someone. "Thanks, Demitri." Then I hear him growl. "What's your name?"

"Cillian Byrne."

"Dam –"

"Do you seriously think you'd be in this car if I didn't know who you were?" Cillian snaps at Damien.

A strangled sound escapes me. Not because of the hostility between Cillian and Damien, but because I keep seeing my father and brother die. The flashes won't stop.

The way their bodies jerked. The blood. The moment they hit the floor.

I was still in shock from hearing Dad contracted Damien and then… my family. My whole family. They're all gone.

I gasp for air as a cry ripples up my throat.

I have no one.

"Poppet," Cillian murmurs as he pulls me tighter to his chest. "I'm so sorry. I've got you. I won't let anything happen to you."

"You can't promise me that." My voice is hoarse from the raw and incessant grief ripping through me.

"Winter," Damien snaps from the front, and my eyes rush to meet his in the rearview mirror. "You're safe. I'll get you home."

Home.

What's the use of having a home if there's no family to fill the walls?

Oh, God.

Another wave of sorrow hits, threatening to drag me under.

Gasping, I lift a hand to my throat as it starts to ache from all the strain of not crying.

Dad. Sean.

Sean.

Oh, God.

A sob pushes past my defenses and escapes my parted lips.

Sweet Sean.

"He's dead," I whimper. "Sean's dead. I didn't protect him."

Cillian's hold on me tightens, and he presses a kiss to my forehead. "I'm so sorry, poppet."

"Blyad'," Damien growls, and then something slams into the back of our jeep.

Pulling away from Cillian, I glance out the back window. There's a black car right on our tail, but I can't see the driver through the tinted windows.

Suddenly, Damien takes a sharp turn up a narrow street, and it has my body falling against Cillian's. "Seatbelt," Cillian mutters, and helping me back to my side of the backseat, he straps me in.

I grab hold of the door and brace myself as Damien swerves around corners. Buildings blur from the speed we're going. My eyes find Damien, and I focus on his tight and secure grip on the steering wheel.

Then it hits again. Damien's my custodian now. Unknowingly, it was the last gift Dad gave me. Probably, the most important gift ever.

The protection of a Vetrov.

Then I remember the call Damien made, and I manage to ask, "Did you speak to Demitri?"

"Yes. He's on his way."

"Alexei?" I ask.

"Yes," Damien grinds the words out.

Revenge.

I'll be able to take revenge with them on my side.

My sorrow morphs into a deadly force, giving life to the strength I need to get through this. I'll avenge my family.

"I want every last Blanco dead," I growl. "I don't care how much it will cost. I don't care how many men you have to hire. Build an army and eradicate the Blanco name."

"Winter," Cillian stops my rant. "First, we need to get back to the island."

I shake my head hard. "I'm done running. It's all I've done my entire life. Run and hide. And for what? I still lost my whole family. Blood for blood. I won't rest until they're dead."

My anger feeds off my grief, becoming an inferno that threatens to incinerate the woman I was. A daughter. A sister.

Blood Princess.

Not because of the diamonds but because I've been soaked in the blood of my family.

"What island?" Damien asks.

"Near Finland," Cillian answers. "We have to find a way to get there. Taking the jet is out of the question. They'll probably have men watching it."

"Blyad'! That's a thirty-five-hour drive. If we don't stop." Damien's voice is tense, and it makes my muscles stiffen.

"We can get a plane in Germany," Cillian voices.

"We need passports. We need to find a place to lay low," Damien grumbles.

I push myself a little up, and glancing through the back window, I see we've lost whoever was following us.

Cillian's phone begins to ring, and instead of handing it back to Cillian, Damien answers, "Yes." He listens for a moment, then asks, "Where?" I watch as Damien looks at the road signs, and then he slams on the breaks. "Thanks. I'll be in touch."

Damien makes a u-turn, and it has Cillian asking, "Where are we going?"

"Friends of my brother," he answers briskly.

We only stay on the road for another ten minutes, and then Damien stops the car in front of a building.

"This is it?" I ask. "It looks abandoned."

Damien grabs the two guns and checks their clips before turning off the engine and opening his door. My eyes dart to Cillian as Damien gets out of the car, and then my door is pulled open. Damien grabs hold of my arm and yanks me out.

"Hey," I snap at him, but he ignores me, and keeping a hold of my arm, he drags me along as he walks toward an old wooden door.

Cillian falls in on the other side of me, grumbling, "You don't have to handle her so roughly."

"Until the twelve months are up, her life is in my hands," Damien snaps as he bangs on the door. "I'll keep her alive my way."

An elderly man opens the door, and it has Damien saying, "Vetrov."

The man stands to the side, and when we walk inside, my eyes widen at all the luxury. Three men are sitting at a table, playing cards. They look like they're all in their thirties. The one gets up and walks toward us. "Damien. Demitri said you would visit. Welcome."

I watch as they shake hands, and the man only spares Cillian and me a glance, then he murmurs, "This way."

As we climb a set of stairs, Damien asks, "Passports?"

"Tomorrow," the man answers.

He opens a door, and we step into a suite. There are two briefcases set on the coffee table, and Damien drags me toward them.

The man helping us shuts the door, and the second we're alone, Cillian says, "Fill me in with whatever you have planned."

Finally, Damien lets go of my arm, and he opens the first briefcase. It's loaded with stacks of euro bills. Seemingly pleased, he opens the second one, and then the corner of his mouth lifts as he glances over the Heckler and Koch P30L, Glock 26 compact pistol, Browning Hi-Power Mark 3, a suppressed gun, and four KA-BARs.

He turns his attention to Cillian. "We'll get passports tomorrow and then get our asses out of Switzerland. Which airport would you use in Germany?"

"Bad Kissingen near Bavaria," Cillian answers.

"We avoid that one." Damien walks to the door, and glancing from Cillian to me, he mutters, "Stay."

When he leaves, I turn my gaze to Cillian. For a moment, we stare at each other, and then he closes the distance between us and pulls me against his chest. It's all it takes for me to break.

Cillian comforts me as I mourn my family, and when I finally find my voice, I whisper, "You're all I have now."

Cillian presses a kiss to the top of my head and rubs his hand in rhythmic movements over my back. "Love you, poppet."

I cling to the man who first took on the role of my mother and now has to take on the role of my entire family. "I can't lose you."

Cillian pulls back, and lifting his hands to my face, he brushes the remainder of the tears away with his thumbs. "If the worst happens and I don't make it –"

I instantly shake my head. "I won't survive without you."

"You will." Cillian grabs hold of my shoulders and locks eyes with me. "You're so brave, poppet. I know you'll survive. I've taught you everything I know. You have the Vetrovs. You're the Blood Princess. You will survive. You'll crush your enemies. You'll become the powerful woman I know you can be."

"Not without you," I squeeze the words out through clenched teeth.

Cillian pulls me back against his chest. "I'll be next to you every step of the way."

"Promise," I whisper as I find comfort in his firm hold.

"Promise, poppet."

DAMIEN

After I get the burner phone from Armindo, I sit down at one of the tables and dial Demitri's number. Armindo places a bottle of Stoli and a tumbler down in front of me then walks away.

"Vetrov," my brother barks.

"It's me. We're in the safe house."

Demitri lets out a relieved sigh. "Carson will meet you there, but he can't stay. He has a job."

"I understand," I mutter as I pour vodka into the glass. "Thanks for the money and weapons." I take a sip and let the drink burn down my throat. "Thanks for everything."

"You're my brother," Demitri grumbles. "Our flight leaves in twenty minutes."

"We're heading to Germany first thing in the morning," I inform him. "Let's meet at Augsburg Airport in Bavaria. It's only a five to six-hour drive from here."

"Okay." He pauses for a moment, then says, "The contract for Adrian Vincent has been issued. Fifteen million euros to whoever kills him."

"Good," I grind the word out. "The fucker took a shot at me."

"He did?" Demitri growls. "He's as good as dead."

I take a long sip of the vodka then say, "Winter wants the Blanco family wiped out."

"How much is she willing to pay?" Demitri asks.

"I don't know. Once you and Alexei join up with us, we can talk business."

"Let her know Alexei is charging five million for coming to help."

"I will."

"Get some rest," Demitri mutters. "I'll see you tomorrow night."

We end the call, and I pour myself another drink. I'm halfway with it when Armindo approaches me. "I need photos. Bring the man and girl."

Nodding, I down the rest of the drink and get up. I take the stairs, and when I walk into the room, it's to find Cillian and Winter sitting on a couch. He has an arm wrapped around her shoulders. Both their heads snap up, and when I see Winter's red-rimmed eyes, it makes the whole night play out in my mind again.

My muscles tighten, and I fist my hands to control the anger swirling in me. I want to rip Adrian's spine from his body for the pain he's caused Winter.

"St. Monarch's issued the open contract on Adrian Vincent. He assassinated your father and brother."

Winter's lips part as the news hit her.

"Alexei's charging five million for coming to help."

She begins to nod. "Okay."

"Clean up," I instruct her. "We need photos for the passports."

Winter goes to wash her face, and it gives Cillian and me a moment alone.

Our eyes lock, and then he says, "Get used to having me around. I'm not leaving her side."

"She's my charge," I growl. "You will do exactly as I say."

Cillian takes a threatening step closer to me. "You will not yank her around. You'll treat her with respect."

Slowly, I shake my head. "Don't tell me how to do my job."

Our eyes remain locked, and then Cillian backs down. Wiping tiredly over his face, he mutters, "What a fuck up."

He can say that again.

"Not exactly the job I wanted," I voice my own thoughts for the first time.

"I didn't know Patrick was going to bid on you. He didn't tell anyone," Cillian informs me.

Winter didn't know?

"It's done," I say as I clench my jaw.

Winter walks back into the living room, looking a little better but still too pale.

"Let's go," I grumble as I walk to the door.

"How safe is this place?" Cillian asks.

"Safe enough for tonight. We leave at four am."

Walking down the hallway, Winter's right behind me with Cillian bringing up the rear.

When we come down the stairs, Armindo gestures to a door next to the bar. "This way."

Walking inside the small room, I go stand in front of a white wall, and Armindo takes a photo.

"Next," he mutters.

Winter goes to stand in front of the wall, and I cross my arms as I watch.

I need different clothes. This suit is becoming suffocating.

When Armindo has the photos, he says, "I'll send food up to your room."

"Thanks."

We head back up to our room, and once we're inside, I glance at Winter. "Take the bed and get some sleep."

She shakes her head and sits down on the couch.

I remove my jacket, and unbuttoning my shirt's cuffs, I begin to roll them up as I take the other couch. I pull the briefcase with weapons closer so I can inspect them.

My gaze lifts to Winter, and our eyes lock.

Day one, and I failed.

We keep staring at each other, Winter with grief darkening her eyes and me with the bitter reality that this will be my life for the next twelve months.

But even in this dark hour, the push and pull is still a constant between us. With my job requiring me to be at Winter's side twenty-four-seven, it's only a matter of time before I claim the debt she owes me.

Chapter 13

WINTER

I don't break eye contact with Damien as I lean my head against Cillian's shoulder and snuggle against his side.

Earlier today, I thought I was saying goodbye to Damien, and now he's here, right in the middle of my hell.

And my life depends on him.

I have the best protection in the world, yet I feel utterly vulnerable. Stripped to the bone. Alone.

No, not alone. I still have Cillian.

My eyes begin to burn from all the staring and the constant fight to keep the tears back. Slowly, I let them drift shut. The last thing I see is Damien's dark brown eyes filled with rage and something else I don't have a word for.

After a couple of minutes, Cillian whispers, "I think she's finally asleep."

There's only a grunt from Damien.

I'm about to tell them I'm awake when Cillian says, "I've been her guard since the day she was born. Winter's the daughter I never had. She's my life."

There's only silence from Damien, so Cillian continues, "She loves horses. Only pictures of them and those little statues. She's scared of the real thing. The one time I wanted to give her a riding lesson, she screamed and scared the shit out of the horse and me." Cillian lets out a soft chuckle, and I feel it vibrate through his torso.

"Why are you telling me this?" Damien asks.

"So you'll see her as a person and not just the Blood Princess." Cillian takes a deep breath. "You probably got to know the strong version of her during training. Yeah, she's a spitfire, but there's so much more to her. She loves with all her heart. When she laughs…" I hear the smile in Cillian's voice, "it comes from her belly. It's loud and infectious."

Oh, Cillian.

I struggle to keep my breathing even as my broken heart squeezes.

"She loves the rain. Always thought the clouds were crying when she was just a wee lass." He lets out another soft chuckle. "She's lived a secluded life on the island.

After her mother's passing, she asked me to train her so she could protect Sean. He was everything to her."

Silence follows Cillian's words, and I can't stop from swallowing hard on the lump in my throat. I can't break down in front of Damien. He's only here for a year, and then he'll leave. Right now, he's my custodian, but a year from now, he might become my enemy.

Cillian clears his throat then asks, "Tell me about yourself. Where did you grow up?"

The seconds stretch long before Damien murmurs, "Russia. The family compound." More seconds pass, then Damien continues, "My uncle took over raising me after my father died."

"Tell me something that makes you human," Cillian says.

This time there's a long pause. "I like the rain."

"What else?" Cillian whispers.

"Enough. I'm not having this talk with you," Damien mutters.

It becomes quiet, and I can only hear Cillian's and my own breathing.

"What's the plan for tomorrow?" Cillian asks.

"We'll leave for Bavaria. It's a five-hour drive. My brother will meet us there."

There's a knock on the door, and I hear Damien get up. Seconds later, he lets out a breath of relief. "Carson. Come in."

Cillian shifts as I lift my head, and glancing over my shoulder, I watch as Carson walks into the suite. His eyes meet mine, and with a slight nod, he murmurs, "My condolences." He turns his attention back to Damien and hands him a bag. "I figured you'd need this."

"Thanks."

Carson follows Damien to the bedroom, and they're in there for a while.

Cillian brushes his hand over my hair. "You need to get some sleep, poppet."

I shake my head and let out a sigh. "I can't."

Just as he pulls me into a hug, there's another knock at the door.

Cillian gets up and opens for Adrmindo and an older woman who brings food and water.

I'm not hungry either.

Cillian shuts the door then calls out, "The food's here."

There's no answer from the room. Cillian brings me a plate and a bottle of water before getting his own.

I stare down at the stew, and it makes my stomach churn. Bending forward, I place the plate on the coffee table, and then I open the bottle and drink half the water. It cools my aching throat.

The bedroom door opens, and Damien comes out, dressed in black cargo pants and a shirt that spans tight over his muscled chest.

He murmurs something to Carson before letting him out, and then he picks up the last plate of food and water. When he takes a seat across from us, he keeps his eyes lowered to his plate.

"What did Carson say?" I ask softly, not having the energy for anything louder.

"Nothing of interest to you," Damien mutters before he drinks some water.

A foreign sensation creeps through me. I don't want Damien here if he doesn't want to do the job, but I know I'll die without him. It feels like I'm stuck between a rock and a hard place, and they're threatening to crush me.

Getting up, I walk to the bathroom, and when I shut the door behind me, I still and stare blankly at the tiles.

Dad's dead.

Sean's dead.

They're gone, just like that.

The grief slithers around my heart in a death grip, and lifting my hands, I cover my mouth to mute my rapid breaths.

I try but fail to keep the tears back.

DAMIEN

I watch as Winter wraps her arms around herself as she tries to rub some warmth into her thin arms.

Getting up, I walk to the room and grab my bag with the clothes Carson brought. I carry it to the living room and take out a sweater. I toss it to Winter, then open the briefcase with money and load it into my bag.

"Are we leaving?" Cillian asks as he rises to his feet. He stretches then stares at me.

"Yes." I take the Glock from the other briefcase and hand it to him. Picking up the Heckler and Kock, I hold it out to Winter.

"Thanks," she murmurs as she gets up to shove it into the waistband of her pants at her back. My sweater is too big for her, and the sight of her wearing my clothes makes my body warm from the inside out.

I attach a KA-BAR to my belt and take the Browning and suppressed gun for myself. The extra ammo is loaded into the bag.

"Let's go," I mutter as I head for the door. Winter sticks to my back with Cillian behind her as we go down to the ground floor.

Armindo glances up from where he's sitting at a table. "Ready?"

"Yes."

He holds a set of keys and the three passports and other ID documents out to me. "I got rid of the jeep. The SUV you'll use is parked at the back. There are extra plates in the passenger door compartment."

"Thank you," I murmur as I take the keys and documents from him.

We follow Armindo through a series of hallways until we reach the back door. He opens and checks if it's clear, then stands aside so we can pass by.

"Thank you," Winter whispers as we leave the building.

Reaching behind me, I take hold of her hand and yank her right to my side. "Stay next to me at all times. I don't want to have to look for you when we're attacked," I grumble as we walk to the SUV.

Cillian opens the back door, and it has me saying, "You're driving. I need both my hands-free."

"Okay." He takes the keys from me and opens the driver's door.

I climb in next to Winter and set the bag down between us.

Only when Cillian starts the engine do I say, "Schaffhausen. We'll go to Augsburg Airport from there."

"Got it," Cillian mutters as he pulls away from the pavement.

The streets are quiet, which is good. I check the passports and hand Winter hers.

She sets it down on her lap, then she glances at me, and our eyes lock.

I can see the questions in her gaze, and knowing we have to talk about the future, I murmur, "Tell me about the island. The layout. The security. Everything."

"It's seven hundred acres," she begins. "A forest of birch and pine covers the land. We have security cameras and motion detectors set up all over the grounds. There are four piers, a helipad, and a landing strip with a hanger for a small jet or aircraft."

When she swallows, my gaze drops to her throat before meeting her eyes again.

With all hell breaking loose, my attraction for her took a back seat, but as Cillian drives us out of Switzerland, it begins to sink in that Winter is under my protection. I have twelve months with her.

"There's a swimming pool covered with camouflage netting and enough housing for a small army. We're also equipped with our own satellite dishes."

I nod, memorizing the information. "How many guards?"

"Twenty-three," Cillian answers. "All trained by me."

"Good," I murmur while my eyes leave Winter to scan our surroundings.

Just outside Zurich, Winter asks, "Will Alexei be able to get more men?"

"Yes."

"We're meeting him and Demitri today?" she asks again.

"Yes."

"Thank you," she whispers, and the sincere tone in her voice has my eyes snapping to her.

I miss seeing the spark of fire in her gaze, but I understand she's taken one hell of a blow with the loss of her family.

When we drive through Zurich, I say, "We need to hide the weapons. If they pull us over at the border, we're fucked. Find an underground parking."

A few minutes later, Cillian steers the SUV into an underground parking area. As soon as he parks the vehicle, I hold my hand out to Winter. "Gun."

She hands it over, and I get out. Opening the passenger door, I wiggle the panel loose and let out a relieved breath when there's space. I grab the gun from Cillian as well, and he has to help me put the panel back on.

"What about the knives?" Winter asks.

"Under the spare wheel," Cillian says.

Nodding, we move to the back as I mutter, "Bring the KA-BARS from my bag, Princess."

When she joins us at the back, there's a slight smile tugging at her lips.

She likes it when I call her princess?

At first, it was a derogatory name, but it's grown on me since.

Cillian lifts the mat, and we tuck the knives under the wheel. "Hopefully, we won't be searched," he mutters as we close up.

We pile back into the car, and then Cillian steers us toward Schaffhausen.

As we near the border control post, there are several cars on the road, which gives us better odds of not being pulled over and searched.

Winter clamps her hands together on her lap and pulls her bottom lip between her teeth.

"Don't look nervous," I murmur to her.

When I'm able to see border security, my eyes stay glued to the man. My breaths slow down, and my muscles tighten. When we're in sight of him, I reach for Winter's hand.

Her gaze snaps to mine and then down to my hand covering hers.

"Smile. You look like you're about to have a panic attack," I say as a smile forms around my own lips.

Instantly her mouth curves up, and it's just in time.

We look normal.

I keep my eyes on hers as we drive over the border, and Cillian lets out a relieved breath when we're not stopped. I pull my hand away from Winter's and scan our surroundings as we drive into Germany.

One obstacle down. Many to go.

Chapter 14

WINTER

After passing the border between Switzerland and Germany, we stop to fill the tank and retrieve the weapons.

When I start walking toward the restroom, Damien snaps, "You go nowhere without me."

Glancing back at him, I say, "Fine. Hurry up. I need to use the restroom."

Things have been weird between us since he became my custodian. I actually miss the friction that kept me on my toes. It's gone because there's nothing to fight him on. Everything he does is to keep me alive, and I'm not about to jeopardize it by being difficult.

Damien stalks toward me and grabs hold of my arm. I yank back against him, a scowl forming on my forehead. "You don't have to drag me, Vetrov. I'm not stupid."

Much to my surprise, the corner of his mouth lifts, and he lets go of my arm, only to place his hand on my lower back.

Was he trying to get a rise out of me?

As we walk toward the restroom, I become highly aware of Damien's hand on my back. It makes the familiar tingles I always feel in his presence come back, and for the first time, I welcome it. It chases some of the suffocating grief.

How did we get to this moment? I have a merciless killer on my side. Yesterday morning he was still an enemy, and now he's all that stands between my enemies and me.

Which means, once more, I'm in his debt.

"I owe you too much," the words slip from me before I can stop them.

"Your father paid for my protection," he mutters.

Dad.

God, how will I survive without my father? I know nothing about the business. Sean was the one being trained to take over.

The new panic robs me of my breath. I don't even know what the family's finances look like. Dad paid twenty-five million for Damien. I owe Alexei five million.

"What's wrong?" Damien asks as we reach the restroom.

"Nothing," I whisper. Walking inside, I find a stall and shut the door behind me. I stand still and take a couple of deep breaths.

We just need to get back to the island. I'll be able to look at the finances then. Cillian will know what to do with the business. He can show me how to run it.

The thoughts calm the panic, and I quickly relieve myself. Washing my hands, I look at my reflection in the mirror.

I look awful.

I look like an orphan.

I look weak.

Lifting my chin, I take a deep breath.

Once I'm home, I can grieve. Until then, I have to be the Blood Princess, the last living Hemsley.

When I step out of the building, Damien's right by the entrance. Again he places his hand on my lower back as we walk to the SUV.

Reaching the vehicle, Damien removes the knives from the back, and it gives me a moment alone with Cillian.

"Do you know anything about running the business?" I ask.

Cillian nods. "I'll show you the ropes as soon as we're home. Don't worry, poppet."

"And the finances?" I ask.

Cillian shakes his head. "I know who the accountant is. We'll check with him."

"Let's go," Damien mutters, and we all climb back into the car.

Cillian starts the engine, and as he steers us back onto the road, Damien curses, "Fuck, that's a scout. Ninety meters behind us."

I start to turn, but Damien places his hand on my arm. "Don't. Let them think they have the upper hand of a surprise attack."

He pulls his phone out, and after dialing a number, he says, "We're going to come in hot. We just picked up a tail."

He listens for a moment, then murmurs, "Yes. Da! We're two hours out."

When Damien ends the call, his gaze snaps to Cillian. "If they catch up to us, we just need to make it to the airfield."

"Won't they be able to shoot the private jet down before we even take off?" I voice my worry.

"There's a hanger. We need to park in it. Demitri and Alexei will wait there to help take out the threat before our plane takes off."

My body tenses, knowing we're in for a rough morning.

Damien reaches out to me, and for a moment, I think he's going to take my hand, but instead, he places the Heckler and Koch on my lap. I instantly grab hold of the gun and check the clip.

Damien opens his bag and hands me two more clips.

Lifting my butt off the seat, I tuck them into the pocket of my pants.

I watch as he checks his own weapons and Cillian's gun before handing it back to him.

"Everyone ready?" he asks.

"Yes." Cillian's answer is clipped, all his focus on the road.

Damien turns his gaze to mine. "Just do as I say."

I nod and check my gun again. After a long hour and a half, the hair on the back of my neck prickles from not looking behind me. I sit frozen, my eyes darting over the scenery I can see.

It's only a matter of time.

Will they attack instantly or follow us to our destination?

Suddenly Cillian curses, "Fuck. Here they come."

Damien glances behind us, and then he lets down his window. Cillian does the same, and it has me opening mine as well.

Damien grabs hold of the back of my neck, and then I'm shoved down on top of his bag. "Stay down. This car isn't bulletproof."

I move down into the foot space between the seats, and it earns me a nod from Damien.

My heartbeat begins to speed up as the seconds tick by.

My mind clears off all grief, of all worry, and for a blessed moment, it's silent inside of me.

"Brace yourselves," Cillian snaps.

They slam into the back of our car, and it instantly makes my blood rush through my veins.

Damien braces his right knee on the back seat and positions his gun between the two headrests.

"Stay down, poppet." Cillian's words aren't even cold when the first spray of bullets shatters the back window.

Damien ducks and then starts to return fire.

More glass shatters, and our car lurches forward as we take another bump from behind. With my eyes glued to Damien, my fingers tighten around the gun, my finger ready on the trigger.

Damien takes another shot, and then squealing tires fill the air.

"Nice shot," Cillian compliments him.

Damien is quiet and tense, never taking his focus off our enemy.

Our enemy.

With bullets flying and death ready to feast, the realization fills every part of me.

I have Damien Vetrov. I have the best custodian.

"Five minutes out," Cillian mutters. "Just five minutes."

The sound of gunfire increases, which means their reinforcements just joined.

"Call Demitri," Damien growls at me. "Tell him we're close."

I move a little up and grab Damien's phone from where it was lying on top of his bag, and press redial on the last number.

"Where are you?" A vicious growl comes over the line.

"It's Winter. We're four minutes out."

"One jeep, two SUVs, and a sedan," Damien shouts.

"Did you hear that?" I ask Demitri.

"Yes. We're ready. Go straight for the hanger."

The call ends, and I toss the phone back on the bag. "Demitri says they're waiting in the hanger."

"Got it," Cillian grinds out as he takes a sharp turn.

My body falls back between the seats, but Damien doesn't move at all as he keeps returning fire.

"I see it," Cillian shouts, relief bleeding into his words.

Damien sits back down, and keeping his head low, he reloads his weapons. His eyes lock on mine. "You do not leave my side."

I nod quickly.

"Get ready," Cillian grits the words out between clenched teeth, and then he swerves sharply, bringing the SUV to a sudden stop.

Damien opens my door, and yanking me up, he pushes me out the door. As he climbs out behind me, bullets spray into the other side of the car.

Heavy fire is returned and glancing to my left and right, immense relief washes over me when I see Demitri and Alexei.

"Go!" Demitri shouts.

Damien grabs hold of my arm, and then I'm yanked to my feet as we begin to run.

Glancing over my shoulder, I watch as Cillian stays by the SUV to help take out the enemy. We rush through wide doors, and then Damien slams my back against the steel.

When he moves into the open and begins to fire shots, I peek around the door. I watch as one man after the other falls.

My eyes go to Alexei, who's taking them out with a grin on his face.

Mother of saints. He looks like death itself.

As my gaze turns to where Demitri is, I latch onto Cillian, who's positioned between them. It's only for a second, and then his body flies back.

A scream rips from me, and I dart forward. I feel Damien's fingers claw at the sweater I'm wearing, but I'm too fast for him. Lifting my arms, I begin to shoot as I run toward Cillian. A bullet whizzes past my head, and I take down three men in the short distance and then drop to my knees next to Cillian. He's gasping for air, and his eyes instantly lock onto mine. "Poppet."

I press both my hands to the wound in his chest. "Cillian," I gasp. His blood seeps through my fingers, and I push harder to try and stop it. "God, Cillian."

No. No. No.

Horror begins to crash over me, threatening to drown me in unbearable pain. I watch the last person who means the world to me struggle to breathe, and it makes something shatter inside of me.

The gunfire stops, and then Alexei shouts, "Get your asses on the plane."

With a lot of effort, Cillian lifts a hand to my cheek, his touch weak. "Love you, poppet."

A sob ripples up my throat, my eyes never leaving his. "It's okay. You're going to be okay," I begin to ramble, my voice quivering with naked fear.

Cillian slowly shakes his head. "Go. You need to... get out of... here."

"I'm not leaving you," I cry, pressing harder on his chest.

Cillian's breath begins to rattle, the sound the most horrible thing I've ever heard.

"N-no."

Damien wraps his arm around my waist and begins to pull me away from Cillian. "Wait!" I cry as I fight against his hold. "Wait!"

Cillian's lips curve up in the lopsided grin I love so much, and then he breathes, "Pop... pet."

Damien yanks me up against his body and begins to carry me away. I watch as the light dims in Cillian's eyes and his breathing stills, and then the distance between us grows fast as Damien carries me away.

"No!" I scream, devastating grief ripping through me. "Cillian!"

DAMIEN

Winter fights against my hold as I make a run for the plane. "Stop!" I shout at her, but she's beyond the point of rational thinking.

Fuck.

I drag her up the stairs, and once we're safely inside the plane, I push her down on a seat. She instantly darts up, and I have to force her down. Her eyes look feverish, her breaths too fast.

"Winter," I snap to get her attention. Her eyes dart to mine, but only for a second. I manage to strap her in, and taking the seat next to her, I wrap my arms around her to keep her seated.

A whimper ripples over her lips, and then a silent cry tears through her. The sounds stab at my heart, the emotion foreign. Never has anyone affected me the way she does.

Seeing her pain makes me want to kill. It makes an untamed possessiveness claw through my chest.

Her body keeps jerking, and she feels small and broken in my arms. Moving one hand behind her head, I push her face against my neck. Her breaths burst against my skin as she gasps through her sorrow.

Unable to stop myself, I press a kiss to her hair. My eyes find Demitri, where he shuts the door. Alexei instructs the pilot to take off, and then they both take a seat across from Winter and me.

I don't let go of Winter. Deep down, I know I'll never be able to let go of her. Instead, my gaze stays locked on my brother, whom I haven't seen in months.

Only when we reach altitude do I slacken my grip on Winter. Bringing my hands to her cheeks, I lift her face to mine. "I'm sorry."

She keeps gasping, her features torn with grief. Her pale skin and the crushed look in her eyes make her breathtakingly beautiful. It makes me want to rip my chest open so I can hide her there from the world.

I didn't know the man well, but anyone could see the love between Winter and Cillian was special. She could cope with her father and brother's deaths, but I'm not so sure about Cillian's.

Winter gasps one more time, her eyes locked with mine, and then she stills. It looks like she switches off, and her features relax into a grim expression.

Slowly, I pull my hands back, and when she doesn't dart up but instead slumps against the seat, I pull the phone from my pocket. "Here are the coordinates," I say as I get up. I hand the phone to Alexei, and as he takes it, our gazes meet.

A slow grin spreads over his face, and then he pulls me into a hug. "Little fucking shit. Good to see you."

I pat his back, and even though the atmosphere is loaded with Winter's grief, I still chuckle.

Alexei pulls back, and I turn to my brother. We stare for a moment, and then similar smiles spread over our faces as we grip hold of each other.

Thank God.

Now we can stop running and plan our retaliation.

"Missed you," Demitri murmurs.

"You too."

When we let go of each other, Demitri glances at Winter. "How's she holding up?"

I turn my eyes to Winter's pale face, a blank expression in her eyes.

"Not good. She lost everyone."

"She's still alive," my brother mutters, and when I turn my attention back to him, he grins, "Not bad for a first day's job."

Alexei comes back from the cockpit after informing the pilots of coordinates. He brushes past us then takes a seat opposite Winter. I sit down next to her and Demitri across from me, and then I watch as Alexei stares at Winter.

Slowly she lifts her head and settle her eyes on his.

"Blanco. You want revenge," Alexei gets right down to business.

"I want them eradicated," she grinds the words out.

"Your island. Is it guarded?"

"Yes," I answer on her behalf. I tell them everything I've learned about the security.

"We'll need our own men for an attack," Demitri voices.

"Get on it," Alexei orders him.

While Demitri starts making calls, Alexei pins Winter with a brutal look. "My condolences."

She only nods slightly, her jaw tightening.

God, this woman is something else.

Is she even human?

Then again, I'd probably react the same to Demitri dying. First revenge, then I'll grieve.

"Tell me about the diamond business," Alexei orders.

Winter shakes her head, and then it looks like she realizes something bad as her lips part. "I... I know nothing. My brother was going to take over. Cillian... Cillian..." her voice grows hoarse as it fades.

The news makes Alexei's lips curve, then he murmurs, "I'll help for a price."

"How much?" Winter asks, her eyes settling on him again.

"I'll let you know."

I can see Alexei's mind working behind his dark eyes. His gaze snaps to me, and then his smile grows. "Not bad for your first contract. I'm proud."

I only nod, then turn my attention back to Winter. My eyes scan over her, and seeing her bloody hands, I unfasten her seat belt and pull her up. I lead her to the restroom and opening the faucets, I hold her hands beneath the water, washing off Cillian's blood.

Standing close to each other quickly fills the air with an intimate feeling, and I glance at her face. Winter's eyes meet mine for a second before lowering to the basin.

For the first time since I've met her, she looks vulnerable. Up until now, I wasn't allowed to feel anything for Winter. But for twelve months at least, she's mine.

Having her so close to me, the anticipation begins to wake my body and heart. After I pat her hands dry with towels, I pull her to my chest and wrap my arms around her.

She stands frozen, and it has me murmuring, "I'm sorry for your losses."

"I want them all dead," she whispers, lifting her hands to my sides. I feel her grip hold of my shirt, and then she rests her cheek against my chest.

Winter... vulnerable and totally dependant on me.

This is what I craved. To have her at my mercy. I just didn't want it to happen this way.

I pull a little back, and placing a finger beneath her chin, I nudge her face up until her eyes focus on mine.

"We'll kill them all," I promise. "By the time we're done, you'll truly be the Blood Princess."

My Blood Princess.

Fire sparks in her eyes, and determination settles hard on her face. "No. I'll be the Blood Queen."

God, still so fierce.

It makes everything I felt for her at the academy return with a force. I'd love nothing more than to claim her mouth and taste the fierceness on her tongue but now's not the time.

I'm going to claim the payment she owes me once we're on the island. She will warm my bed during the nights, and in return, I'll kill her enemies.

I will own her body, her broken heart, her unwavering spirit.

I'll help her take her rightful place in her family's business while satisfying my craving for her.

Chapter 15

WINTER

Stepping off the plane, the ground feels foreign beneath my feet. A month ago, this was home. Everything was familiar.

Now it's a reminder of what I've lost.

I keep my head held high as I walk to the mansion. The front door opens, and Dana, the housekeeper, begins to smile until she sees the three men behind me. Her eyes dart back to mine, and I see the questions form on her face.

I stop in front of her and shake my head. "It's just me. They're dead."

Dana's lips part with shock, and unable to care about her feelings, I start to walk toward the stairs. I climb them with heavy feet, and only once I turn down the hallway, and I'm out of sight, do I stop again.

The devastation of the past twenty-four hours pulverizes my heart into a bloody mess in my chest.

My feet begin to move, and I find myself opening Dad's bedroom door. My eyes scan over his belongings, and it increases the incessant ache in my chest.

He was mostly gone on business throughout my life, but the time we did spend together was priceless.

I take the key out of the lock, and pulling the door shut, I lock it. I walk to Sean's room, and this time I step inside.

God, I can still smell him.

I pick up the shirt lying next to the laundry basket and stare at it.

I'm so sorry, Sean.

My chin begins to quiver as tears blur my sight. Before they can fall, I set the shirt down and walk out of the room. I lock the door, not wanting anyone in their personal space.

Glancing to my left, my blurry sight focuses on Cillian's door.

Every muscle in my face tightens as sorrow overwhelms me. My feet find their way to his room, and when I push the door open, a soft sob floats over my lips. I step inside and shut the door behind me. Slowly, I glance over his trinkets, and his favorite coat draped over the back of a chair.

There's only one framed photo on the bedside table. It's one Mom took. Cillian and I are walking across the backyard at our property in Ireland.

Seeing him, so young, his posture straight and ready to protect me breaks the last of my willpower. A tear spirals over my cheek, and taking a quivering breath, I glance around his room. My eyes land on his stereo system, and moving closer, I check what CD he has in.

The Wailin' Jennys.

I select *The Parting Glass* and press play.

As their harmonious voices fill the air, I close my eyes, and the tears start to fall.

Cillian.

You were supposed to be with me until the very end.

My protector.

My friend.

Since my first memory, you were there. Every day.

You loved me more than anyone.

How am I supposed to do this without you?

You didn't teach me how to live without you.

My sorrow engulfs me as my shoulders begin to jerk, and I allow myself to mourn the loss of the person I loved above all else.

As the last chords of the song play, I whisper, "Goodnight, Cillian."

The door slams open behind me, and I glance over my shoulder as Damien stalks inside Cillian's sacred space.

"I told you to never leave my side," he growls at me.

I turn to face him, but everything in me is too raw.

Damien's eyes drift over my face, and then he closes the distance between us and yanks me to his body.

Everything in me wants to rest my head against his chest, but knowing I can't, I push against him and glare up at him. "I don't need your pity."

His eyes lock with mine, and they don't seem as cold. "You've suffered an unspeakable loss, Winter. This isn't pity. This is me showing you, you're not alone. You have my loyalty."

"Your job description doesn't include comforting me," I murmur, still trying to regain control over the sorrow.

Damien just stares at me, and then he slightly tilts his head. "This isn't just a job for me. I have a personal interest."

I begin to nod, letting out a humorless burst of laughter. "Right. The debt I owe you."

"Damien. Winter," Demitri calls from the hallway.

"Here," Damien answers as he steps away from me.

Not wanting them in Cillian's room, I turn off the stereo and walk out into the hallway. As soon as Damien steps out of the room, I pull the door shut and lock it. I pocket the three keys, then turn to Demitri.

"Alexei wants to talk," he mutters.

Damien waits for me to follow after his brother, and as we walk down the hallway, I begin to feel on edge.

Both the Vetrovs and a Koslov are in my home. Pins and needles slowly spread over my body when I realize my life depends on the most dangerous men in the world.

I have no one on my side. The void Cillian and my family have left has changed my entire world.

Demitri leads us to the dining room where Alexei's taken my father's place at the head of the table. His deadly eyes lock on me, and I stop on the other side of the long table.

"Sit."

Demitri takes a seat on Alexei's right. When I remain standing, Damien places his hand on my lower back, giving me a soft nudge.

I shake my head. "I'll stand."

This is it. This is where Alexei makes his demands, and there's nothing I can do. He has all the power.

"I'll help," he begins.

"What's your fee?" I ask, not knowing if I can even afford him. Maybe if I sell the island or the property in Ireland? But it can take months or even years to find a buyer and to free up the money.

Alexei's eyes slowly drift between Damien and me, then he says, "A partnership." A slight frown forms on my forehead, but before I can say anything, Alexei continues, "If I have an interest in your business, it will give me the incentive to protect it."

My mind begins to race. I did not expect him to say that. "How much?" I manage to ask.

"Fifty percent."

God.

Will I be selling my soul to the devil if I agree?

I need them more than they need me, though. I don't have much of a choice. I know nothing about the business. I need their protection. I need someone to show me the smuggling routes. I can't deal with the tribes on my own. They'll probably kill me during the first meeting.

Alexei rises to his feet, and with his eyes burning on me, he says, "I want an alliance, and you're in no position to decline."

I know. God, I know.

"Fifty percent of your business for the protection of the Vetrovs and the Koslovs. You'll be untouchable. Your business will survive. You have everything to gain."

Everything he says is the truth. I have no choice, but I can't bring myself to open my mouth even though I have no other option but to agree.

"A marriage between you and Damien." Alexei's words don't register at first.

"What?" the word drifts over my lips.

"A marriage," Alexei repeats as he begins to walk toward me. "An alliance between the Hemsleys and the Vetrovs. Damien gets half of the business. He'll run it on my behalf once we've taken care of your Blanco problem."

A marriage?

To Damien Vetrov?

Mother of saints.

Slowly I turn my gaze to Damien, and my eyes flit over his face. He looks impassive as if it's not his life we're talking about as well.

Alexei lets out a dark chuckle, "Surely you weren't raised thinking you'll marry for love?"

"Of course not," I bite the words out. "It's just… sudden. I need time to consider it."

Alexei slowly shakes his head. "Time is not a luxury we have. Do you agree or not? I need to know if I'm staying or going home. Time is money."

My heartbeat matches the seconds as they pass. My eyes go to Demitri's expressionless face, then back to Alexei's dark stare.

I'll have the Vetrovs and Koslovs on my side for life. I've lost all the love in my life, but I can buy the loyalty of these men.

My lips part, and then the words leave me, "I agree."

The corner of Alexei's mouth lifts, and then a smile spreads over his face, and somehow it makes him only look more terrifying. "Congratulations, brother. I bargained a wife for you."

"Thank you," Damien replies, not sounding upset at all.

"Are we done?" I ask, needing to get away from their intensity and demands. I need to think. I need to process.

"For now," Alexei murmurs.

Without sparing any of them another glance, I leave the dining room.

I have no idea what my future holds except that Damien will be at my side every step of the way. Not out of love but because of self-interest.

The alliance has been made.

The price of their loyalty is the cost of the four lives I've lost. Cillian. Sean. Dad. Mom. They all died for the business, and now only half belongs to me.

DAMIEN

Alexei chuckles at Winter's quick retreat from the dining room, then his eyes settle on mine.

"I saw the way you looked at her. I figure this deal is a win for all three families. You're good?"

I nod. "Yes."

I'm more than good. Alexei just gave me everything. A formidable business to help me take a seat of power in The Ruin and the woman I've wanted to claim since the first moment I saw her.

There's only one problem. Winter looked indifferent about the alliance. As if I'm nothing to her, and it doesn't sit well with me.

"I want this marriage officiated before we do anything to help her. I'll arrange for an Orthodox priest to come here. Tomorrow."

"The sooner, the better," I agree. "Thank you, Alexei." My eyes go to my brother, and seeing the pride on his face fills my heart with a burst of warmth.

I leave the dining room and heading up the stairs, my body tenses, and my eyes narrow. Winter better not think this will be a marriage in name only.

Over my dead body.

Turning down the hallway, I see Winter rush into a bedroom and follow after her. I shove the door open, and it has her quickly turning to face me. Stalking into her bedroom, I spare the luxurious furnishings nothing more than a glance before locking eyes with her. For seconds we stare at each other.

Winter lifts her chin in defiance, the spark I've become addicted to igniting in her emerald irises.

"You're not happy?" I ask as I slowly step closer to her.

Her features tighten. "I agreed to the alliance. Happiness has nothing to do with it."

I stop several inches from her. "The marriage will happen tomorrow. Alexei won't help unless we're legally bonded to each other."

"I figured as much," she mutters.

Lifting my hand to her neck, I wrap my fingers around her throat and brush my thumb over the scar. I feel a tremble ripple through her body, and it pleases me.

Leaning down until I feel her breath on my face, I murmur, "Don't make the mistake of thinking this marriage will be in name only."

Her eyes widen at my words. "You expect it to be real?"

"Of course." The corner of my mouth lifts. My words are low and unyielding as I say, "The payment I demand for the debt you owe me is your body, your heart, and your soul."

Winter's breaths begin to speed up, her expression tightening with defiance. "I will never bow before you," she grinds out through clenched teeth.

Her statement makes my lips curve higher. Fighting with her is exhilarating. The fire in her eyes makes heat pour through my body. It feeds my addiction and makes me want to claim her this instant.

"Oh, you'll kneel before me, Princess," I whisper darkly as I close the distance between us. Before she can react, I crush my mouth against hers in an unforgiving kiss.

Winter freezes, and when she doesn't push me away, I allow my lips to caress hers, my teeth to tug at her bottom lip, and finally, for my tongue to dive into her warm depths.

The moment I taste her, I lose control. I wrap a hand around the back of her head, and my fingers tighten their grip around her throat, effectively keeping her in place.

Tilting my head, I ravish her mouth, sucking hard on her tongue and plundering her lips.

Then she moans. *She fucking moans.*

And I know I've won.

I break the kiss, and pulling back an inch, my eyes seize hers in a captive hold. Winter's lashes are lowered, her cheeks tinged with pleasure, her swollen lips parted and ready for more.

My mouth curves up in victory as I murmur, "Judging by how your body is trembling for me and how eager you are to accept my tongue, our wedding night will be anything but in name only."

Tomorrow night I'll claim every inch of her. The Blood Princess will be mine in every way.

I watch as shock darkens her eyes, and then she yanks against my hold on her neck. For now, I let her go, and she quickly puts a safe distance between us. As if that will stop me from taking what I want.

The fear returns to her eyes, and like a depraved predator, I feast on it.

"Today, you mourn your loss. Tomorrow we'll marry, and it will be consummated." I take a step closer to her again, and it makes her body stiffen. "And then I'll kill your enemies."

My last words make the fear retreat from Winter's eyes. Lifting her chin, she says, "I have requests of my own."

I tilt my head slowly and cross my arms over my chest. This should be interesting. "Let me hear them."

"If the marriage is consummated, I won't stand for a parade of other women through my house."

Ahhh... my princess is possessive. I don't think she knows what she just gave away with that request. It tells me she cares enough to not want to share me.

Slowly, I nod.

"I want Alexei to teach me everything about the business. I demand to be present for every meeting. I will not have the three of you push me aside to take full control."

"Naturally," I mutter.

"And I want to kill Antonio Blanco."

Which means she wants to go with us when we attack. For a moment, I hesitate, not wanting her in harms way, but then I relent, "You have to follow my orders during the attack. You have to stay by my side."

Winter nods.

"Anything else?" I ask.

"You will treat me with respect, and I will do the same. If you raise your hand against me, I will kill you in your sleep."

Her words make my lips curve up. I begin to move slowly toward her, and when she doesn't step back to avoid me, it makes my heartbeat speed up. My eyes claim hers, and as I lean down, I murmur, "The only thing I'll raise for you is an empire, built on the bones and blood of your enemies."

"Good," she whispers, her breaths starting to come faster.

I lower my head more until we're breathing the same air. "Treat me like your king, and I will make you a queen."

Her eyes search mine for the truth of my words, and when she finds it, she pushes up on her toes, pressing her mouth to mine.

Submit to me, and I will burn the world down for you.

As if she can hear my thoughts, Winter lifts her arms, and wrapping them around my neck, she parts her lips. Her tongue slips into my mouth, and then I take over. I push her back until she's pressed against the wall.

My body cages hers in and my hands lift to her cheeks. I hold her in place as I deepen the kiss, drinking from her mouth like a man dying of thirst.

Moving a hand behind her head, I pull the hair tie out, freeing her hair. I grip a fistful of the silky strands as my tongue thrusts into her mouth, giving her a taste of what I intend to do to her tomorrow.

My blood rushes through my veins, and I'm swept up to great heights from the taste of her. This woman who never backs down. Who walked into the academy to show her enemies she's a force to be dealt with. Who made me want more than just to be a custodian.

Yesterday, I cursed Patrick Hemsley for bidding on me, and today… today I'm taking over his empire. Tomorrow I'll take his daughter.

Chapter 16

WINTER

Damien's mouth on mine clouds my mind. It eases the unrelenting ache in my chest. It erases my worries about my uncertain future. Until there's only him. His aftershave. His strength pinning me to the wall. His fingers in my hair. His tongue stroking mine with a dizzying pleasure. With a single kiss, he awakens my soul. He makes my heart race and my body tremble with need. Need for more of him.

I knew Damien was a force to be reckoned with, but still, I underestimated him.

I knew the Vetrovs and Koslovs would want more than I was willing to offer. That's how it works in our world. But still, I didn't know Damien wanted me. Not like this. Not so desperately that his kisses bruise my lips and his tongue creates a fire in my mouth.

God. Damien Vetrov.

Tomorrow he'll become my husband.

He breaks the kiss, and all I can do is stand breathlessly plastered against the wall.

Tomorrow we'll consummate our marriage. I'm no stranger to sex, but… but… Lifting my eyes to meet his, I take in the hunger darkening his face. The dominance pouring off him.

I've always been in control whenever I had sex, but I know with dead certainty it won't be the case with Damien.

He brings his hand to my jaw, and his thumb brushes over my swollen bottom lip. His voice is a low rumble as he says, "Mourn. Tomorrow will be a new day."

I stay against the wall as he turns away from me and leaves, and only when the door shuts behind him do I take a deep breath. I press a hand over my racing heart, trying to calm it down.

Tomorrow I'll marry Damien, and I'll become Winter Vetrov. The name alone will inspire fear. Alexei, Demitri, and Damien will help me run the business.

It will only cost my body, heart, and soul.

I'll be entirely at Damien's mercy.

The thought both scares and thrills me.

With Cillian by my side, I always had someone to look out for me. Will Damien fill that void in my life?

No. He'll be loyal to me, but the chances of him loving me are probably next to zero.

Being loved died with Cillian and my family. Loyalty will have to be enough for me.

Pulling away from the wall, I walk to the bathroom and opening the faucets, I let water pour into the tub while I go to my closet to get clean clothes.

Thankfully, I left half my belongings at home when I left to attend St. Monarch's. Taking a pair of sweatpants and a t-shirt out, I go back to the bathroom.

It's only when I've stripped out of the dirty clothes, and I sink into the balmy water, that my thoughts turn back to the past twenty-four hours.

Seeing my father and Sean being assassinated right before my eyes shocked me to my core. But watching Cillian die was unbearable.

I begin to remember the precious times I had with him. I remember when he trained me. When he taught me how to dance. When he showed me how to ride a bike.

Cillian is in every single memory that matters to me.

But now he won't be in my future.

The grief thickens around me, and I allow the tears to fall. One last time.

Like Damien said, today I mourn, and tomorrow I have to face a new life. As his wife.

I move slowly as I wash my body and hair, grateful for the alone time Damien's given me.

The shock and sorrow keep hitting me in waves. The severe losses I've suffered. How my life has changed and how much it's still going to change. Everything feels foreign. Even my body.

Getting out of the tub, I dry myself and lather my skin with lotion. I pull on the clean clothes and then towel dry my hair.

I'm still squeezing the last water from my hair as I walk to my personal living room when I see the tray on the coffee table. There's a plate of food and a glass of cranberry juice.

I still don't have an appetite, but I'm going to need the strength for tomorrow.

I sit down and drop the towel on the side of the chair and then force myself to eat the chicken and vegetables Dana must've prepared.

I need to talk to the staff. God, there's so much to do.

When I drink the last of the juice, I go back to the bathroom and pull a brush through my hair. Leaving it to air dry, I slip on a pair of sneakers and then leave my room.

Luckily there's no sign of the men as I take the stairs down. I find Dana in the kitchen, where she stares out the window with a far-off look.

"Dana," I murmur to get her attention.

Her gaze snaps to me, and then she rushes to where I'm standing. She hugs me tightly. "I'm so sorry, Miss Winter."

I nod as she pulls away. "Our guests will be here a while. Two of them might come and go but the third…" I swallow hard then break the news to her. "I'm marrying Damien Vetrov tomorrow."

Her eyes widen, the legend of their name known amongst the staff as well.

"Is it a good arrangement?" she asks.

"Yes. It's the best option for me under the circumstances."

Her eyes widen again, and then she says, "We have a lot to prepare for tomorrow."

"I'll take care of everything," Alexei suddenly says behind me. "Consider it a gift."

I swing around, so my back isn't to him. His eyes drift over me, and then the corner of his mouth lifts. "You look better." Then his gaze moves to Dana. "We'll eat now."

"Yes, Mr. Koslov," she murmurs fearfully and gets back to work.

Alexei pins me with his stare, and it has my feet moving. As I walk by him, he says. "After we've eaten, join me in your father's office. We need to talk business."

I nod and then head to the front door, needing to escape the men who seem to have made themselves right at home.

Walking through the birch and pine forest toward the shore, my mind races, jumping from all I've lost to my impending marriage to Damien.

I wish Cillian was here. Then I wouldn't be in this position. Losing him tore a gaping hole through my heart and life.

God, and it leaves me totally at Damien's mercy.

The thought shudders through me again, and it makes me walk faster as if I can flee it.

As I reach the shore, I stop, my breaths rushing over my lips. My gaze finds the town in the distance, and I stare until my sight blurs. My thoughts turn to the past month and how everything has changed.

The first time I saw Damien, and learning he's a Vetrov. The shock and fear I felt. The training sessions and seeing how good he is. Unbeatable. Too strong for me to stand a chance against him.

My breath shudders over my lips, and my eyes drift shut against the brutal reality of what my future holds.

I remember how angry Damien was when my father won the bid.

It's only with this thought that I realize Damien's life has also changed. He's stuck with me and probably trying to make the best of the situation.

Still, the marriage won't be in name only. He made it clear he wants everything. Yes, the attraction has always been there, right from the first time we met, but I wasn't sure whether he felt it too.

He took it easy on you during training.

He helped you during the laser game.

It wasn't my imagination when we almost kissed!

The realization has my eyes snapping open.

Damien fought Vince and Hugo for me and guarded me while I was drugged.

My breaths begin to speed up again.

Damien wants me as his wife. He wants my body, my heart, my soul.

God. That gives me all the power I'll need to survive in this world. If I can make him love me, then I'll truly become untouchable.

He said if I treat him like a king, he'd make me a queen.

For the first time since my life shattered into an unrecognizable mess, do I feel a glimmer of hope shine through the darkness.

Before I can wage war against the Blancos, I'm going to have to wage war for Damien's heart.

I'll use what he wants as a weapon. I have to make him worship me.

I take a deep breath, filling my lungs with the fresh air.

I have to attempt the impossible because I don't even know if Damien is capable of loving anyone.

DAMIEN

I watch as the small army of staff Alexei arranged for the wedding, scurries in and out of the house, getting everything ready for the ceremony that's scheduled to happen at sunset.

Shaking my head, I glance at where Demitri is watching the spectacle while enjoying a tumbler of vodka.

"Leave it be, brother," he mutters. "It's tradition. After the ceremony, Winter Hemsley will be family. She'll be a Vetrov. It's something worth celebrating."

She'll be mine.

Nodding, I leave Demitri and head up the stairs to check on Winter before getting ready. I've left her alone the entire day but need to make sure she'll go through with marrying me. When I open her bedroom door, there's a buzz of low voices, and Winter's surrounded by women tending to her hair and makeup.

The women gasp when they notice me, and then Winter turns her back to me. "I'm sure this is bad luck, and I don't need any more of that. Get out."

"You'll be ready in an hour?" I ask as my eyes scan over the silky robe she's dressed in. The silk following the curve of her body makes her look more petite.

It's only a matter of hours until I claim her.

"I'll be ready," Winter answers.

"Good," I mutter. "Because I'll drag you to the priest if I have to." I pull the door shut and walk to the room I've taken for myself, so I can get ready. After showering, I put on a black tuxedo.

God only knows how many lives Alexei threatened to make this wedding happen so fast.

When I'm ready, I take a moment to breathe. Closing my eyes, I inhale deeply. I'm still adjusting to the sudden change of direction my life took. I was trained to be Carson's custodian, but that's no longer my future.

Instead, Winter Hemsley will be mine within the hour.

As I open my eyes, the corner of my mouth lifts. With the thought that I'm going to enjoy taming her wild spirit while taking charge of the diamond smuggling industry, I leave my room.

I find Alexei and Demitri in the dining room, where they're talking to the priest. The table and chairs have been moved out, and the walls have been covered with Russian religious art.

When my gaze lands on the two traditional crowns set on a side table, the moment becomes real.

"Damien," Alexei calls me out of my thoughts. I walk closer, and after I'm introduced to the priest, I move to the side of the room with Demitri by my side.

"You're sure about this alliance?" Demitri murmurs.

I nod as I fold my hands in front of me, my eyes glued to the doorway. "I am."

"I'll go get the bride," Alexei says, and then he walks out.

It's only then I feel a flutter of excitement.

This is it.

Minutes crawl by before Alexei appears in the doorway, and as he steps inside, it gives me a clear view of Winter.

My lips part as her beauty rips the air from my lungs. Her hair is covered with a lace veil. Slowly she lifts her head, and then our eyes meet. Everything fades until there's only her.

The white wedding dress hugs her chest and waist before flaring out around her hips. I don't know what fabric it's made of, but it's perfect. It sparkles like a million tiny diamonds.

Demitri nudges my back, and it makes me move forward. Reaching Winter, I hold my forearm out to her, and she places her hand on my arm.

"You look exquisite," I murmur before I lead her to the priest.

The ceremony begins, and even though it must be foreign to Winter, she keeps up. The priest takes the rings Alexei got us, and holding them in his hand, he makes the sign of the cross. "The servant of God, Damien Vetrov, is betrothed to the handmaid of God, Winter Hemsley, in the name of the Father, and of the Son, and of the Holy Spirit."

Taking the rings from the priest, Winter and I exchange them while vowing ourselves to each other. When I slip the golden band onto her finger, the corner of my mouth twitches.

We're given candles to hold, and again the priest reads from the scripture. Afterward, he chants a psalm, and then he reaches for the first crown. I press a kiss to the crown and then bow my head. Winter follows my lead as the priest crowns us king and queen of our own kingdom.

"The servants of God, Damien Vetrov and Winter Hemsley are crowned in the name of the Father, and of the Son, and of the Holy Spirit."

I take hold of Winter's hand and place it on top of the priest's, who then leads us around the room as we take our first steps as husband and wife.

The priest removes the crowns while praying and then gives us a final blessing. "On behalf of the church, I wish you both many years of blessings and grace as you delight in your love for one another, a love that finds its source and fulfillment in God Who is love itself."

It's done.

Alexei comes to hug me, pressing a kiss to my cheek. "Congratulations, brother."

While Alexei moves to Winter, Demitri pulls me into a tight embrace. "You've made me proud."

"Welcome to the family, Winter," Alexei says, a smile spreading over his face. "Now we drink."

Turning to Winter, the corner of my mouth lifts. When she raises her chin, and our eyes lock, I murmur, "My wife."

"Husband." Hearing the word drift over her lips makes the blood rush through my veins.

I close the distance between us, and wrapping a hand around the back of her neck, I murmur, "It's tradition to kiss your husband."

I lower my head, my eyes locked with hers, and then press my mouth to hers.

Now to get through the toast so I can take her up to the bedroom and consummate this marriage.

Chapter 17

WINTER

Damien keeps giving me penetrating stares as if he's trying to see into my mind. Every time his eyes lock on me, it makes a shiver rush over my body.

I feel a little anxious about us consummating the marriage. I'm used to being in control, and I don't think it's something Damien will stand for in the bedroom.

"A toast," Alexei says as he raises his flute filled with champagne. We do the same, and then he says, "To alliances, family, and loyalty."

Demitri and Damien repeat the words, and then Alexei looks at me, and it has me saying, "Oh, yes. Alliances and loyalty."

"And family," Alexei murmurs darkly, his eyes locking with mine.

Family.

The word creates a sharp ache in my chest, but still, I force it over my lips, "Family."

I take a sip of the champagne, and as the conversation turns to the grounds, how many guards there are, and when the other men will arrive, I set the flute down on a table and walk out of the room.

If we're going to talk business, I'm not doing it in a wedding dress. I take the stairs up, and as I enter my bedroom, I wonder if Damien will move into this room now that we're married or if he'll want separate bedrooms.

Stopping in front of the dressing table, I take out the earrings and pull the veil off. I remove all the pins from my hair and let out a tired sigh as I pull my fingers through the strands. All this dressing up and effort for one hour.

I walk to my closet and kick off my shoes, and then I freeze. I feel Damien, but listening closely, there's not a sound from him. Then his fingertips brush over my bare shoulder blades, and it instantly makes goosebumps burst over my skin.

Just a touch. That's all it takes from Damien to make me tremble.

"You're not staying to talk business?" I ask, keeping my voice soft.

"That's what tomorrow is for," he murmurs.

My stomach begins to tighten with nerves, and my breathing speeds up.

Damien's hand moves down, and I feel him fiddle with the back of the dress.

"Thank you for looking beautiful today." His voice is a soft caress that makes my heartbeat speeds up until it feels as if it's fluttering in my throat.

Damien tugs at the dress's strings, and I feel as the pressure of the fabric begins to give way. Not wearing a bra, I'm left standing in my panties as the wedding dress drops to the floor.

Deep breaths, Winter. You can do this.

Remember, he already wants you. Half the battle is won.

I swallow and then step out of the dress and turn to face Damien.

His eyes sweep slowly over my body, then back up every inch before settling on my face. His brown irises darken to midnight black, and he clenches his jaw as if it's taking all his self-control to not just fuck me.

Ravenous. That's how he looks. Like a predator that's about to devour its prey.

God.

I close the distance between us and then lift my hands to his belt. Damien tilts his head when I begin to unfasten it, and when he doesn't stop me, I unbutton his pants and pull down the zip. When my knuckles brush over the hard outline of his cock, I almost freeze.

I take a slow breath, and keeping my eyes locked with his, I lower myself to my knees.

My pride takes a blow as I tilt my head back, and I see the corner of his mouth lifting.

"Kneeling before me, princess? So soon?" he murmurs, his voice laced with warning.

It's a bitter pill to swallow as I go against what I told him yesterday, that I'll never bow before him.

Look at me now.

I shove the thoughts aside.

Focus.

"You're my husband," I explain as I begin to pull the fabric open, exposing black boxers to me.

"Get up," he grumbles as I take hold of his boxers, my knuckles brushing over the hard muscles of his abdomen.

I shoot a glare up at him, then snap, "This is where you want me, is it not?"

This time his lips curve higher as he replies, "I'm curious to see how far you're willing to go with this façade."

All the way, if it means I'll have you kneeling at my feet by the time I'm done blowing your mind.

I pull the fabric down, and Damien does nothing to stop me as I expose his cock to me. Unable to stop myself, I lower my eyes until I come face to face with his thick hard length. Velvet skin stretches firmly over his large cock, the veins snaking from the base to the crown, making it look like a merciless weapon.

I let out a breath, and when the hot air hits his erection, Damien lets out a hiss. "Enough. Get up."

Ignoring his order, my lips part, and I lean forward. As I suck him into my mouth, Damien's body stiffens, and he twitches against my tongue.

Up until now, I've been too anxious to feel anything else, but as I begin to suck him deeper, my abdomen tightens, and my core flushes with heat.

"Princess," Damien growls, and hearing the tight restraint in his voice makes me smile around his thick length.

I pull back and slowly brush my lips over the crown before swirling my tongue around his girth.

"Blyad'." The word is nothing more than a whisper, and I notice how he fists his hands at his sides.

I suck him back into my mouth, and wanting to weaken him, I begin a relentless pace, my head bobbing forward. I only manage to take half of him and wrap my fingers around his base, squeezing hard.

"Fuck." Damien's hands shoot forward to my head, and for a moment, I think he's going to push me away, but instead, his fingers fist in my hair, and he yanks me against him until the crown hits the back of my throat. I almost gag, and it makes my eyes instantly tear up.

I keep sucking hard, hollowing my cheeks, and it doesn't take much longer before warm liquid spurts down my throat. Damien's hips jerk, and his hands tighten their grip on my hair as low grunts escape him.

I swallow it all and slowly pull him from my mouth. Licking my swollen lips, I climb to my feet and meet Damien's burning gaze with a defiant stare.

DAMIEN

I struggle to bring my breathing under control from the intense orgasm I just had. I've had blowjobs before, but nothing like that. Maybe it meant so much more because it was Winter, the princess who refused to bow before anyone… until today.

I don't like that she took control. Not one bit.

Pinning her with a murderous glare, we stare at each other, neither of us willing to back down.

She might be used to being in charge in her own life, but I won't tolerate it in the bedroom.

Seeing the defiance in her emerald gaze only makes me more determined to tame her. Grabbing hold of Winter, I shove her back onto the bed. I begin to yank the tuxedo from my body as my eyes rake over every inch of her exposed skin.

She's a fucking goddess.

I rip my shirt off and make quick work of my pants and underwear while kicking my shoes off. When I'm finally naked, Winter's eyes roam over my body, and her breathing begins to speed up as her green irises darken with a hungry look.

Placing a knee on the bed, I take hold of the white lace panties and drag them down her legs. When she's totally naked, my eyes lower to the neat strip of ginger curls.

Winter begins to move, trying to sit up, and it makes me grab hold of her shoulders, pinning her down to the mattress. "Keep still," I growl the instruction as I keep myself braced over her.

The expression on her face turns to a glare. "I'm not going to lie still like a docile submissive."

Her fight makes my lips curve up, and then my mouth crashes against her.

"You will submit," I growl against her lips before I bite her bottom lip and suck on it.

She tries to turn her face away from me, and it has me wrapping my fingers around her throat.

Winter grabs hold of my biceps, her nails digging into my skin, and then she pushes her body up against mine. Unlike before when we were in training, and I subdued her, feeling her bare breasts pressing against my chest makes me lose control.

I begin to ravish her mouth, my tongue brushing hard strokes against hers. Winter doesn't submit one bit but matches my strokes with her own.

Wanting to gain the upper hand, I slip my other hand between her legs as I partially lie down over her. When I spread her open and my middle finger presses against her clit, her body jerks, and she gasps into my mouth.

Not giving her a moment to grow accustomed to my touch, I begin to rub hard circles around the sensitive bud.

Winter's breaths start to rush against my lips, and lifting my head, I capture her eyes, filled with an inferno of heat.

My voice is low as I say, "Submit."

"No," she gasps, every muscle in her body tightening beneath me.

I increase the pressure on her clit, and without any warning, I thrust a finger inside her. Her inner walls instantly clench around me, trying to suck me deeper. I pull my finger out and return to punishing her clit until her features begin to tighten.

"Come, Princess," I murmur, my voice deep with the need to see her lose control.

Her grip on my biceps tightens, and then her body begins to shudder as a whimper escapes her lips.

She doesn't look away as her orgasm hits. Instead, Winter keeps her eyes locked on mine. Her lips part with a moan, and then her body bows against mine.

Pleasure strips the defiance from her face, and I'm rewarded with soft moans as she rides out her orgasm against my hand.

When her body slumps back against the bed, my lips curve up into a victorious smile.

"Two can play this game," I murmur as I lean forward to claim Winter's mouth so I can feel her breaths rush over mine. "You can't win, Princess. Not against me."

Chapter 18

WINTER

I must be sick because it's one hell of a turn-on to fight Damien in bed.

The corner of my mouth lifts as I push against him, trying to get him onto his back. The man is a mountain, though, and I quickly give up.

It makes him chuckle into my mouth before his tongue sweeps over mine. Feeling his naked body pressing against mine makes me tremble for more.

The kiss grows rough until my lips are tingling from the friction. I move my hands to Damien's chest and slowly brush my palms over his skin as I drink in the feel of every rippling muscle.

His body. God, his body. Just looking at him in all his naked glory was enough to make my ovaries go up in flames, and now I get to touch him.

By the time I reach his abs, I'm almost drunk on the feel of him. I keep going lower, my fingers dancing over the chiseled curves of his hips. My temperature spikes, and I'm in danger of overheating as I flatten my hands over his ass.

Damien reaches down, and grabbing hold of my thighs, he yanks my legs open. Instantly his hard length settles against my pulsing core.

My mind clouds over with lust, and I whimper into his mouth. In return, his teeth tugs at my bottom lip, and he presses his cock hard against my sensitive flesh.

The trembling in my body grows as I pass the point of fighting for control. I just want Damien inside me.

God, fuck me already.

Instead of getting what I want, Damien breaks the kiss, and locking his burning gaze with mine, he slowly begins to rub his cock against me.

I need more. So much more.

I widen my legs as much as I can, giving Damien full access.

Still, he doesn't thrust inside me but instead sets my body alight with need as he keeps slowly rubbing his thick length against me.

I dig my nails into his ass, and it only makes his lips curve up.

"Submit," he growls, the sound of his low voice making my abdomen clench.

For a moment, the head of his cock flirts with my opening, but then he goes back to stroking my clit.

When I tilt my hips up for more friction, Damien pulls away. His lips brush over the side of my neck until he reaches the scar, and then he sucks hard. I gasp as my fingers move up the wide expanse of his back.

Damien moves lower, placing soft bites over my collar bone and down to my breasts. When his mouth finds my nipple, he sucks it hard into his mouth. There's a sharp twinge before he soothes my pebbled flesh with his tongue and lips. He keeps repeating the action until I'm breathlessly arching myself, shoving my breasts shamelessly into his face.

It makes a low growl build in Damien's throat, and when the sound ripples over his lips, he moves down to my stomach. His tongue lashes at my skin, his teeth nipping as he works his way down to my clit.

My entire body tightens, and my hips bow off the bed as I once again press myself into his face. I grab hold of the back of his head with the full intention of keeping him imprisoned between my thighs so I can ride his mouth until I orgasm. But my strength is nothing compared to

Damien's. He only bites me softly before easily pulling free of my hold and crawling back up my body.

I let out a frustrated groan, making the corner of his mouth lift in a ravenous smirk.

"Submit, Princess," he growls as he braces his body over mine.

I almost give in but manage to shake my head as my eyes drift down his muscled body until settling on his hard length.

I begin to reach for him, but he grabs hold of my hand and pins it down above my head. Shaking his head, he settles himself between my legs and rests his full weight on me.

It feels glorious.

"You want my cock," he murmurs as he nips at my mouth. "Admit it, Princess. You need me to fuck you."

Again I manage to shake my head. Just barely, though.

As punishment, his hips rock forward, his erection rubbing my clit into a frenzy.

With my free hand, I grab hold of his ass again, but Damien takes that hand too and effortlessly pins it next to the other above my head. With one hand, he keeps hold of my wrists, and with a wolfish grin spreading over his face, he keeps the torment up by rubbing himself against me.

Another frustrated groan escapes my lips, and then my mind loses the battle, and my body takes over.

Lifting my head, I press a kiss to Damien's jaw. "Please." My teeth scrape over his jaw. "Please." I move down his throat and then sink my teeth into the skin over his pulse. I suck hard before lifting my eyes to his. "Please, Damien."

He looks possessed, and I'm ready to beg some more, but before the words can form on my tongue, Damien positions himself at my entrance. He's big, though, and I try to relax my muscles as he rocks against my opening. The moment his head breaks through, he slams into me so hard it shifts my body up the bed.

I can only gasp from the sharp pain, which I didn't expect.

Damien's eyes rake over my face, looking like the demon I feared when I first met him. But now, the fearsome expression makes me want him more.

I want all of him.

It was my intention to make him obsessed with me, but I fear that's no longer the case.

Damien pulls out and lowering his head, his mouth claims mine in a possessive kiss as he drives back inside me. His hold on my wrists tightens until it becomes bruising as his other hand grips my hip.

He pulls out one more time, and then he begins to move like a destructive force. His hard length filling me completely and mercilessly. His body possesses mine. His mouth ravishes my lips. His touch bites into my skin.

Damien claims the debt I owe him.

As he takes my body, my heart, and my soul, there's nothing I can do to stop him.

I begin to whimper into his mouth as his thrusts grow rougher, hitting me so deep. Each time he fills me, pleasure strikes like a lightning bolt.

His body owns mine, and when he growls, "Come, Princess," it listens. I explode beneath him, into an unrecognizable mess only he can put back together.

A cry tears from me as the intense orgasm seizes me, my body convulsing beneath Damien's. His eyes are locked on mine as he takes in the sight of me coming apart because of him.

As the intense pleasure strips me bare, Damien's features tighten, a possessive expression permanently carved into his face.

"Mine," he growls, and then he finds his own release, his body jerking as he fills me.

Pleasure washes over Damien's face, and never has he looked more brutal and more beautiful.

A merciless Russian God, and I belong to him.

"Yours," I manage to gasp, and it has Damien losing his mind all over again.

DAMIEN

I slowly thrust inside Winter, riding the last ripples of pleasure. Being only with whores before Winter, I've never orgasmed more than once. But with Winter, I'm still semi-hard even after three orgasms. My desire for her is unrelenting and inexhaustible. I'll never be able to get enough of her.

As my body stills against Winter's and we stare at each other, one realization stands out above all others – she's mine. The Blood Princess belongs to me and only me.

When she finally submitted, it shifted something inside me. Not only did I claim her, but it feels as if she claimed me as well.

My eyes search hers, and when I see the warmth blossoming in her emerald irises, my lips curve up.

"My little fighter," I murmur, with no intention of getting up.

Winter tugs at my hold on her wrists, and I let go. She brings her hands down, and cupping my jaw, she lifts her head and presses a tender kiss to my mouth. Resting her head back on the bed, her eyes drift over my face as her fingertips brush over my jaw.

A vulnerable expression flits over her features, and it has me asking, "What's that look for?"

She shakes her head, her fingertips moving down to my neck.

"Tell me," I demand.

She resists for a couple of seconds longer, then she whispers, "I've lost everyone that matters to me."

I rest my forearms on either side of her head, and with my eyes locked with hers, I say, "You have me."

She searches my face for the truth in my words, then she murmurs, "Don't die."

The corner of my mouth lifts. "I won't."

With our soft words, our bodies still joined, and our eyes locked, the dynamics between us gradually begin to evolve into something more profound.

This time when our mouths meet, it's not out of desire or my wanting to claim her. The kiss is tender, filled with unspoken promises as we dedicate ourselves to each other.

By the time our lips part, Winter owns more than just my loyalty.

I pull out, and it draws a gasp from her.

"Don't worry, I'm not done with you yet," I murmur.

It earns me a chuckle from Winter. Sitting up, she says, "First, I need food."

I pull her off the bed as I get up, and when I open the closet and Winter sees my clothes, she asks, "You moved in?"

"Of course," I mutter.

"When?"

"During the ceremony." I pull a pair of black sweatpants on and turn to Winter. "Get dressed so I can feed my wife."

My words make her smile before she disappears into the bathroom. When she comes back out, she puts on a pair of sweatpants and a t-shirt, sans any underwear.

I hold out my hand to her, and when she lies her palm against mine, my fingers close tightly around hers. We leave the room, and I'm glad when we don't run into Alexei or Demitri on our way to the kitchen.

I take hold of Winter's hips and lift her to sit on the table. Then I open the fridge and take the chicken leftovers out. I set the plate down next to her, and picking up a piece, I bring it to her mouth. "Open." Winter's lips part, and having her eat from my hand makes heat begin to slither through my body again.

While she chews the bite, I pour us each a glass of water. I set the glasses down next to the plate, then nudge her legs open and move in between them.

"We're heading out on an errand," Demitri suddenly says from the doorway.

Glancing at my brother and Alexei, I ask, "How long?"

"We'll be back tomorrow," Demitri answers. His eyes move between Winter and me, then he mutters, "Enjoy your wedding night."

I watch them leave, then turn my attention back to Winter.

"We have the house to ourselves tonight," she mentions the obvious.

I pick up another piece of chicken, and holding it to her mouth, I say, "You better eat. You're going to need the strength."

Her lips curve in a daring smirk as she takes the bite. Our eyes remain on each other as I feed her until she says, "Thank you. I've had enough."

Taking hold of one of the glasses, I press the rim to her lips, and as she drinks, some spills down her chin and neck. I lean forward, and starting at the curve of her neck, I lick the wet trail to her mouth.

Setting the glass down, I move my hands to Winter's hips and yank her against me. As her lips part, my tongue sweeps inside.

Our first time together was getting her to submit to me. Now, it's purely about pleasure. I want to enjoy her body.

I begin to thrust against her, the fabric stopping me from taking her too fast.

Brushing my hands up her sides, I pull her shirt over her head and drop it to the floor. My gaze lowers to her chest, and I drink in the sight of her perfect breasts, pebbled hard for me.

I brush my knuckle over her nipple, and the corner of my mouth lifts as she responds with a sharp breath.

Lifting my eyes to hers, I say, "You like having my hands on your body."

"Yes," she breathes.

I palm her breast and watch as her lashes lower over her eyes before I murmur, "Good."

I begin to knead her flesh until her breaths are rushing over her lips.

Closing the last of the distance between us, I press my forehead to hers. "Do you want me to fuck you, my Princess?"

She nods as her hands find my hips.

"Beg."

Winter's eyes burn on mine, and as an incentive, I rub my cock against her again.

Finally, she relents. "Please fuck me, Damien."

Hearing her say the words makes a possessive growl build in my chest as I thrust harder against her. I push her to lie back on the table and strip the sweatpants from her body.

Keeping my own on, for now, I take hold of my cock through the fabric and press against her opening. Her need for me soaks through the material as I push hard to enter her with the head of my cock only, the fabric stopping me from going any deeper.

Winter lets out a throaty groan, and when she tries to reach for me, I grab hold of her hands again, pinning them down on either side of her head. With my upper body braced over her, my eyes drink in the need tightening her features as I begin to thrust with short strokes.

Her breaths begin to explode over her parted lips as I keep stretching her opening.

"Damien," she gasps, and when I only grin at her, she tries to free her hands from mine.

That's right, Princess. Fight me.

I grow impossibly hard, my balls aching as she squirms beneath me.

Her body begins to quiver, and knowing she's close to finding the release she so badly wants, I pull away from her.

This time she lets out a frustrated growl as she glares at me. "Fuck me!"

I free my cock from my pants and position it at her entrance. "Who do you belong to?"

"You," she grinds the word out, her breasts swelling and falling with every breath she takes.

"Who do you belong to?" I ask again as I tease her opening with the head of my cock.

"Damien Vetrov," she gasps.

I slam into her as hard as I can, and it rips a cry from her as her body bucks up. I don't give her time to adjust and set a relentless pace as I fuck her until she's a quivering, whimpering mess beneath me.

I feel my own pleasure creep closer, and bite the command out, "Come, Winter."

She shatters with a scream, her body convulsing helplessly as the orgasm provided by my cock ravishes her.

It makes me reach my own climax, and with hard thrusts, I empty myself inside her.

I slip an arm beneath her and pull her up until we're chest to chest and breathing the same air. When her eyes focus on mine, I growl, "You belong to me, Winter Vetrov. Try and leave me, and I'll kill you because death is the only way you'll get away from me."

Instead of looking at me with fear, she gives me a daring look as she lifts her chin. "Same goes for you."

Chapter 19

WINTER

When I wake up, Damien's not in bed. I sit up and rub the sleep from my eyes. He kept me up until the early morning hours, and I can still feel him inside me.

A smile forms around my lips as I climb off the bed and walk to the bathroom. I open the faucets so the water can fill the tub while I brush my teeth.

Mrs. Vetrov.

I knew our first night together would be intense, but damn, Damien wasn't joking when he said he's going to claim me.

And I relished every second.

Turns out instead of destroying me, Damien's lifting me up out of the ruins left of my life.

I rinse my mouth and then lift my eyes to my reflection in the mirror. I'm no longer the Blood Princess. Last night Damien made me his Blood Queen.

Warmth spreads through my chest, and then I realize I'm falling for him. Fast and hard. At first, the thought makes fear slither through my heart, but then I remember how he claimed my body, and it quickly retreats.

Damien might be merciless, but only when it comes to the enemy. He's a devastating potency no one can escape. Not even me.

I no longer want to escape him. I no longer fear him.

I know with absolute certainty I made the right decision when I married Damien, and it makes me want to get to know everything about him.

I step into the bath, and as I begin to wash my body, I take in the marks he left between my thighs. Love bites are scattered over my breasts.

God, the man branded me.

Another smile forms on my lips as I continue to clean myself. I soak my stiff muscles for a short while and then get out. After drying myself and applying my favorite cherry blossom scented lotion, I get dressed in black cargo pants and a shirt. I pull on my boots, and tying my hair back, I go in search of my husband.

I only find Dana in the kitchen, and while she fixes me a cup of coffee, I stare at the table where Damien made me beg for him to fuck me raw.

"Mr. Vetrov and the other two are out back," Dana informs me as she hands me the steaming cup of coffee.

"Thank you." My gaze drifts over her face, and knowing she must still be hurting, I give her shoulder a squeeze. "We're safe with them," I assure her.

She nods, her blue gaze meeting mine. "You're my family."

"You won't lose me as well," I murmur. "Damien can protect me."

She nods, and I drink half the coffee before setting the cup down. I walk out the backdoor, and glancing over the grounds, I see Damien walking toward me.

"What are you busy with?" I ask when he's close enough to hear me.

Damien doesn't answer me immediately but instead wraps his fingers around my throat, pulling me in for a kiss.

"Morning, Wife," he murmurs against my lips.

"Morning, Husband," I chuckle, but it quickly fades when I see his grim expression. "What's wrong?"

Damien drops his hand to mine, and linking our fingers, he pulls me in the direction he just came from. "Alexei and Demitri got word Adrian was sniffing around Finland. They went to meet with him."

"What?" I gasp. Instantly anger begins to bleed into my chest, and I yank back against Damien's hand. "Why would they meet the man who murdered my father and brother?"

Damien tightens his hold on my hand. "To kill him."

The words wash the anger from me, and I immediately calm down.

His eyes meet mine with a hard stare. "They got him to talk. He was contracted by Antonio Blanco."

"But Alexei killed Adrian? Right?" I ask to make sure.

"He did," Damien mutters as he leads me in the direction of the birch and pine forest.

This is what happens when you marry into the right family. They take care of your problems.

After a couple of minutes, Damien tugs me to a stop. His eyes drift over my face and seeing the worry tightening his features, I ask, "What else?"

"Madame Keller sends her apology. Alexei and Demitri went to retrieve your father and brother's remains last night. As well as our belongings."

His words are a blow to my broken heart, and I struggle to get the words out, "They're here?"

Damien pulls me against his chest, and placing a hand behind my head, he presses a kiss to my hair. "They are. It's time to bury them."

A funeral.

I get to lay Dad and Sean to rest where Mom was buried. My family will be reunited in the afterworld.

The thought gives me some comfort, but it also makes my sorrow engulf me.

When I nod, Damien keeps an arm around my shoulders, and tucked against his side, we walk the last of the distance to the family cemetery.

When we break through the lining of trees, my eyes scan over the two holes, ready for the burial. Seeing the guards who've been with us for years reminds me of Dana.

"Dana should be here," I whisper.

"I'll get her," Demitri offers, and he immediately jogs away.

My gaze stops on the two coffins, and knowing Dad and Sean are inside them makes sorrow twist my heart into a painful lump.

Alexei comes to stand in front of me, and it has me bringing my eyes to his.

"Thank you," I say, my voice hoarse. "Thank you for killing Adrian and bringing them home."

Alexei surprises me by pulling me into a hug, and for a moment, I stiffen in his arms. Then he murmurs, "I tried to find Cillian, as well, but the scene was cleaned before my contact got there."

Oh, God.

Cillian.

What happened to his body? Ugly thoughts begin to swarm in my mind that he was dumped or burned with the rest of the dead.

My shoulders quake under the onslaught of grief, and it makes Alexei tighten his hold on me.

"I'm sorry, little Winter," Alexei whispers.

I nod against his shoulder, and the moment he lets go of me, I step closer to Damien's side.

Damien wraps his arm around me, and I press my cheek to the side of his chest as I try not to cry.

DAMIEN

When Demitri returns with Dana, I lower my mouth to Winter's ear. "Would you like to say something?"

She nods and then steps out of my hold. My eyes don't leave her as she walks to the coffins. Her fingers brush over the wood, and then she asks, "Which one is Sean?"

Alexei gestures to the other coffin, and Winter goes to kneel by it. She swallows hard and presses a kiss to it. "I'm sorry, Sean. I'm so sorry I didn't protect you."

She closes her eyes, and her body jerks once as she fights to keep her emotions under control.

I fist my hands at my sides, so I don't rush to her side. After making her mine, it creates a vicious storm inside me to see Winter in so much pain. My jaw tightens as the need for revenge begins to form in me.

Winter gets up and goes to kneel by her father's coffin. "I'll kill them all. I promise." She swallows hard, then whispers, "Give Mom a hug from me."

She rises to her feet and glances between the two coffins, and then she takes a quivering breath. Softly, she begins to sing, her Irish accent more evident than ever. The guards, who are Irish, softly join in.

The song is the same as the one she was listening to right after we got home. It's filled with reverence, and the love Winter has for her fallen family makes each lyric sound achingly sad.

When the last notes of the song fade, Winter whispers, "Goodnight."

She begins to walk away from the coffins and passes right by me. When she keeps going, I glance at Demitri, who quickly says, "We'll bury them. Go with her."

I rush after Winter, and when I catch up to her, she lets out a heartbreaking sob as she wraps her arm around her middle as if the sorrow is threatening to tear her in half.

Without giving it another thought, I sweep her up into my arms and continue to walk toward the house.

"The shore," she squeezes the words out, and as I change direction, she wraps her arms around my neck and buries her face against my shoulder.

"Shh…" I whisper.

When I reach the shore, I sit down and position Winter, so her back is resting against my chest. I keep my eyes trained on the land in the distance so she'll have some privacy while she grieves.

"Cillian," she gasps. "I can't even bury him."

I wrap my arms tightly around her and press a kiss to her hair. As my wife breaks down in my arms, I promise to make the Blancos suffer the way she's suffering.

Knowing it will help calm her a little, I murmur, "We'll take our revenge soon."

She begins to nod, then turns a little so she can see my face. I take in her tearstained cheeks and the bruised look in her eyes, and once again, I pull her to me.

My arms keep tightening around her until she lets out a whimper. When I slacken my hold, she presses closer to me.

I press my mouth to her forehead as I fight to restrain the incessant need to kill her enemies.

My enemies.

Bringing my hand to Winter's chin, I nudge her face up until our eyes meet. "You're not alone."

Winter nods, and wrapping her arms around my neck, she straddles my lap and presses herself hard against me. I position a hand behind her head and wrap my other arm around her. For a long while, I give Winter the comfort she needs as we just hold each other.

She's grown quiet, but I don't move. As a breeze picks up, she whispers, "I'm falling for you. Please catch me."

I pull back so I can see Winter's eyes, and my gaze drifts over her face. My heart expands until it's brimming with my devotion to her. I've never felt such strong emotions for another person, and it has me murmuring, "I've already caught you. Give your heart to me, Princess. Love me."

Winter pulls her arms back and frames my jaw with soft palms. We stare deep into each other's eyes, and then she leans forward and presses a tender kiss to my mouth. "You have my heart, Damien."

I don't let her pull back but hold her to me as I take her mouth. My tongue brushes over hers, wanting to taste the words she said. Our lips fuse together, and minutes pass while our tongues dance before we slowly pull apart.

Winter rests her cheek on my shoulder, and I feel her breaths skim over my neck. After a couple of seconds, she whispers, "Tell me about your childhood."

Frowning, I ask, "Why?"

She lets out a chuckle. "Growing up, I heard scary stories about the Vetrovs. Cillian made it sound like you're the boogeyman."

"Baba Yaga," I murmur. "Cillian wasn't wrong."

Winter lifts her head and frowns at me.

I glance out over the water. "I fired my first gun at the age of seven. By the time I was thirteen, I never missed. For my sixteenth birthday, my father took me hunting."

"What did you hunt?" Winter asks.

I turn my eyes back to her. "My father had a contract to assassinate someone, and he had me do it."

"So, you killed the contract?" she asks.

I nod, then ask, "How old were you when Cillian taught you to fire a weapon."

"Fourteen."

I lift my hand to her neck and brush a finger over the scar. "Tell me what happened."

Winter takes a deep breath. "We were leaving a shopping center. Halfway to the car, they opened fire on us. My mom… she grabbed me and pushed me to the ground. We both got shot, only she was shot in the head. Cillian grabbed me and got me out of there. He fixed me…" her voice drifts away, and long seconds pass before she murmurs, "Cillian was everything to me. He took over the role of my mother. He was my best friend. He's every good memory I have."

I brush my thumb over the scar again. "You loved him a lot."

"More than anyone."

Our eyes meet, and tilting my head, I say, "I'm sorry you lost him."

We sit for a while longer, then I get up and pull Winter to her feet. As we walk back to the house, I look at the island with new eyes. This place is now my home, and Winter is the only thing I live for.

Chapter 20

WINTER

It's both scary and amazing how quickly life can change. I've lost so much, yet gained at the same time.

As I take a seat at the dinner table on Damien's right, I can't ignore how happy I am. My heart aches for my loved ones I've lost, and it will for a long time to come, but Damien... things have changed between us.

I should've known he'd take his vows seriously. The Vetrovs have honor. I just didn't expect him to assume the role of a supporting husband. He consoled me after the funeral. For hours. He made me feel... loved.

My eyes lift to his face, and I take in his handsome features. He's still the same man I met at St. Monarch's. In many ways he's cold, but then there are tender moments. Like when he saved me from Vince and Hugo.

"Why did you help me when Vince and Hugo attacked me?" When Damien's eyes snap to mine, I realize I asked the question out loud.

"Attack?" Alexei asks. "At the academy?"

I nod. "Vince had me drugged, and if Damien hadn't stepped in…"

Alexei's face turns to stone. "The Vetrovs and Koslovs will always protect those who are vulnerable. We don't beat and rape women. They're meant to be treasured."

"So you won't assassinate one?" I ask.

"Not one like your mother," he answers. "I'd assassinate Sonia Terrero. Free of charge."

Dana brings the food, and when I pick up my utensils, I realize Damien hasn't answered me yet. Glancing at him, he slowly shakes his head at me, then he asks Alexei, "When will the men arrive?"

"Two days," Alexei answers.

Lifting an interested eyebrow, I ask, "How many?"

"Six."

A frown forms on my forehead. "So few."

"My six men will be able to wipe out all your men," Alexei explains. "They're good, and we can't fly a hundred people to Italy."

"True," I murmur.

"And the weapons?" Damien asks.

"Luca Cotroni will have them ready when we leave for Italy. He's graciously offered his home to us while we're there."

"The Cotroni's are your ally?"

"They are," Alexei murmurs before taking a bite of his food.

Thank God. That's good news.

The conversation hovers around the impending attack. When we're done with dinner, I gather the plates and carry them to the kitchen. Just as I walk in, I see Dana wiping away her tears. I set the plates down on the table and walk to where she's standing by the backdoor.

"Sorry," she whispers, turning her face away from me.

I wrap an arm around her waist and stare out at the lights coming from the guards' houses.

"How did he die?" Dana suddenly asks.

I turn my gaze to hers. "Who?"

"Cillian." Hearing the ache in her voice, I begin to frown.

Then I see the lost love in her eyes. "You loved him?"

I don't know why I'm surprised. Dana's beautiful with her black hair and blue eyes. And Cillian, he was attractive in his own way with a larger than life personality.

"Yes," she admits, her voice thick with sorrow.

I pull her into a hug. "I'm sorry, Dana." I rub my hand up and down her back. "He didn't suffer long. He took a bullet to the chest." My own sorrow rears its ugly head as I remember Cillian's last moments. "Right before he took his last breath, he smiled that lopsided grin of his."

She lets out a strangled sob, and clinging to me, she mourns the man she loved.

We pull away, and I gesture outside. "Want to go for a walk?"

Dana nods, and we step out into the dark.

"He loved you like a daughter," she murmurs.

"I know."

Dana takes hold of my hand, gripping it tightly. "At least I still have you."

"You'll always have me."

She glances at me, then asks, "Mr. Vetrov… is he as good as the rumors say he is?"

The corner of my mouth lifts. "He's better. He'll be able to keep us safe."

"I hope he'll be a good husband, as well," she whispers.

"He is," I assure her.

"I'm glad." I hear the relief in her voice, then she asks, "Will we stay here when everything is over?"

"Yes. I don't see why we should move. We'll still need the security, and all our memories are here."

"Good, I was worried we'd have to move to Russia or America," she confesses.

"If there comes a day we have to leave, will you come with me?" I ask.

"Always, Miss Winter. I'll follow you to the ends of the world."

We reach the shore, and I stare at the lights in the distance.

"Why do you love looking at the town?" Dana asks.

"It looks peaceful like a fairytale. I imagine everyone there is happily living normal lives. I was always jealous of them. Being able to walk in the streets without the worry of being assassinated. Having friends. Going to parties and on dates."

"Now I understand," she murmurs. "You never had any of that. I'm sorry, Miss Winter."

"It's okay. I had Cillian. I wouldn't change my time with him for any of that."

And I'd give everything if only I could turn back time and stop him from dying.

I feel Damien, but again I can't hear anything. Glancing over my shoulder, I see his shadow next to a tree, silently guarding us while we grieve Cillian.

"He loved his baked beans on toast. Had it every day," Dana reminisces.

Knowing she needs to talk about him, I ask, "Did he know you loved him?"

She nods then her mouth curves up. "Every night, after tucking you in bed, he would come to me. You were more ours than your parents. Our daughter."

After a moment of silence, Dana lets out a sigh. "Let's go back before they come looking for you."

I let out a chuckle. "Too late." As we turn around, Damien steps out of the shadows. He nods at Dana before holding his hand out to me.

I take it, and as the three of us walk back to the house, I drink in the feel of his strong fingers gripping mine. I glance up at his profile, and then it really sinks in.

Damien is my family now. Along with Dana, the three of us will build a new life.

———————

DAMIEN

When we step into our bedroom, I tug Winter to a stop. She turns to face me with a questioning look.

"I saved you because you were already mine," I admit the reason for the question she asked earlier. I just didn't want to talk about it in front of my brother and Alexei.

Her mouth curves up as she takes a step closer to me. "Why wouldn't you fight me during training?"

"Full of questions, aren't you?" I ask as I wrap my fingers around her throat, enjoying the soft feel of her skin.

"Just curious. You were always closed off, and I couldn't read your facial expressions."

"I refused to fight you because you're so small. There's no victory in beating someone half my size."

I brush my thumb over her scar as she asks, "And during the laser game? Did you want to kiss me?"

"Yes, but I also wanted to strangle you for shooting Carson," I mutter, the corner of my mouth twitching at the memory.

"Are you in love with me?" she asks without blinking an eye.

Am I?

My eyes drift over her face, and then I shake my head, and it makes the playfulness vanish from her eyes.

"I'm not sure," I admit. My words make a frown form on her forehead. "Love is a foreign concept in my world. I understand loyalty, desire, hatred, but love…" I shake my head again. "Would I die for you? Yes. Do I want you? Yes. Will I kill anyone who hurts you? Yes."

"What do you feel when you think of losing me?" she asks.

Without having to think about it, I growl, "Murderous."

What would I do if someone took Winter from me?

I'd lose my mind.

My jaw clenches, and I pull her closer until I feel her breath on my lips, and then I admit, "I'm obsessed with you."

Winter searches my eyes before she murmurs, "To me, it sounds a lot like love, Damien."

I consider her words. "Then you're the only one I'll ever love."

Winter pushes against my hold on her throat and presses a kiss to my lips. "I'm obsessed with you too."

I smile against her mouth. "Good."

Suddenly she pulls out of my hold and walks to the bathroom. I hear her open the faucets, and then she goes to take clothes from the closet.

"Don't bother with those. I want you naked next to me every night."

She lets out a burst of silent laughter as she leaves the clothes and goes to bath.

Walking closer, I push the door open and lean my shoulder against the doorjamb. I watch as my wife undresses. When she steps into the tub, I catch sight of the bruises between her thighs.

"I marked you," I murmur.

"You sure did," she chuckles as she sinks down into the water. "And I'm not complaining one bit."

"Good, because I intend to do it again." I move closer and crouch next to the tub. I reach for the loofah and body wash.

"You're going to bathe me?" Winter asks, her eyes following my movements.

"Yes."

As I begin to wash her snow-white skin, she chuckles. "First you feed me, and now this? Why?"

The corner of my mouth lifts. "You don't know why?"

"No. Tell me."

My gaze locks on hers. "I'm making you submit to me."

Defiance sparks in her eyes. "Is it what you really want? For me to be a submissive wife?"

"No. I never want you to lose your fighting spirit. It's what drew me to you. But knowing you'll submit willingly whenever I want you to is exhilarating."

"A turn-on," she murmurs as understanding dawns on her face.

Leaning forward, I wash between her legs. My voice is low with a burning desire. "Yes, and now you need to get out so I can fuck you."

"You need to shower," she gives me a look filled with warning. "You're not getting into bed all sweaty."

I let out a chuckle. "Fine, but get your ass to bed."

I begin to undress as Winter climbs out of the tub and dries herself. Giving me a seductive look as she walks by me, she says, "Don't take too long."

Unable to resist, I slap her ass, and she makes an adorable squeaking sound.

I only take ten minutes to shower, but when I walk into the bedroom, I find my wife fast asleep. My eyes drift over her sexy body, and crawling over her, I press a kiss to her shoulder and another to her temple. Then I whisper, "Slava ne mogut apisat' mayu lyubof' k tebe."

Sleepily, Winter mumbles, "What?"

I lie down behind her and pull her against me. Pressing another kiss to her shoulder, I say, "Words can't describe my love for you."

Fast asleep again, she doesn't hear the translation.

After breakfast, I lead Winter to the barn. While inspecting the grounds, I saw it was set up for training.

"Why are you bringing me here?" She asks as we step inside.

"You're a Vetrov which means you need to fight like one."

Instantly there's a spark in her eyes. "You're going to train me?"

"Yes." She knows how to fire a weapon, so I pull her to the mat, and turning to face her, I say, "When you're faced with an enemy, there's no time to size them up." I begin to circle her, my gaze drifting over her body. "You're not strong enough to go up against a man, but you're quick."

I move a couple of steps away from Winter and meet her gaze. "Attack me."

She immediately assumes a fighting stance, and it has me shaking my head. "This isn't St. Monarch's. There will be no time to take in a fighting stance. Just attack."

Winter darts forward, and I expect her to go for my legs, but instead, her arm wraps around my neck, and the next second she's on my back, her legs wrapped around my waist. She tightens her hold, and I chuckle before I bend over and slam her against the mat. "Good move but instead of the neck, go for the eyes."

Winter nods as she climbs to her feet. Her cheeks are flushed, and the paleness of grief removed.

I dart forward, and wrapping my arm around her neck, I yank her body back against mine. "Free yourself before I choke you."

Winter struggles against my hold, and then her nails dig into my forearm.

"You know that's not going to work on me. Do better," I growl as I tighten my hold on her.

The next moment, Alexei says, "Slam your head into his face."

Winter just reacts, and before her head can connect with my face, I step back, letting go of her.

Alexei and Demitri come to stand next to the mat, their arms crossed over their chests, then Alexei says, "A man has two weak spots. His cock and his face. If you can't knee him, then you either remove his eyes or break his nose. It will buy you time to finish him off."

Winter nods, drinking the information in.

"But," Demitri says as he steps onto the mat, "It's seldom you're faced with only one enemy. What do you do when you're outnumbered?"

"Fight like hell," Winter mutters, making me chuckle.

"You go for the strongest one first," Alexei advises her as he steps onto the mat as well.

Winter moves back as her eyes dart between the three of us, sizing up which of us are her most significant threat. She darts forward, and the next instant, Demitri has to quickly block before she knees him. I begin to laugh from the surprised expression on my brother's face.

Then Winter explains, "Alexei trained as an assassin, and Damien has to sleep next to me, so it left you, my brother-in-law, as the biggest threat."

Her explanation gets even a chuckle out of Alexei, then he mutters, "Good."

For the next couple of hours, Alexei, Demitri, and I train Winter, showing her how to react faster and where to hit to inflict the most damage.

By the end of the training, Winter manages to block my blows, making the worry ease in my chest. I go for her neck, and she avoids my arm, her feet moving swiftly.

"Good," I murmur, making her grin. I stop moving and smile at her. "We're done for today."

Winter eyes me warily, staying a safe distance away. Chuckling, I shake my head. "Training is over." I begin to walk toward the door calling out, "Come, Wife."

Chapter 21

WINTER

After lunch, Alexei glances between Damien and me, saying, "Come with me."

We follow him to my father's study, and there's a sad twinge as I take a seat at the desk where my father spent most of his time whenever he was home.

Alexei opens a laptop and turns it so both Damien and I can see the screen, then he says, "The finances look good."

My eyes dart over the figures and pointing toward the total amount, I ask, "Is that how much I… we have?"

Alexei smirks. "Yes. One point five billion. That's not taking into account the diamonds your father has in the vault."

"Did you get the code to the vault?" I ask.

Alexei shakes his head. "I had to break in. We'll need to get a new vault." He gets up to retrieve a small wooden case, and when he opens it, my gaze drifts over the sparkling diamonds. Alexei gestures to the largest one. "I have a buyer. He'll pay fifty million for this one."

My eyes dart up to Alexei's as it begins to set in that I'll be okay financially. More than okay.

"Thank you, Alexei," I murmur as I glance down at the diamonds.

"Of course," he murmurs. "This is what family is for."

"How do you know what's fake and what's real?" Damien asks as he leans closer.

I use a pair of tweezers to pick up the largest diamond and hold it closer for him to inspect, then I explain. "There are a couple of ways. Personally, I prefer the sandpaper test. If you rub a fake diamond on it, it will be scratched, where it won't do any harm to the real thing."

Damien nods as Alexei closes the case and places it back in the vault. When he takes a seat again, Damien asks, "What do you know about the smuggling routes?"

"There are a couple. None by land. By air, it's fairly easy as Africa doesn't have strict border controls. Our biggest problem will be dealing with the rebels." Alexei's gaze settles on me. "It won't be safe for you to go."

I instantly frown. "I know it won't be safe, but if I don't take a stand, I'll never be taken seriously in this business."

"We'll talk about it later," Damien mutters, and then he changes the subject by asking, "The men are arriving tomorrow morning, right?"

"Yes, we'll leave for Italy as soon as they're here."

Damien rises to his feet. "We have a lot to prepare before we leave."

"Demitri will make sure the jet is fueled and ready," Alexei says, and when he rises to his feet as well, I do the same.

I watch as the men leave, anger starting to simmer in my chest.

I won't sit on the sidelines while Damien makes the runs. I refuse to.

I walk out of the office and grab hold of Damien's arm before he can take the stairs down with Alexei. He turns to me with a questioning gaze.

I wait until Alexei's gone, then say, "You will not do the runs without me. I told you I won't be some docile wife that sits with my hands folded at home."

Damien's eyes sharpen on my face, and he takes a threatening step closer to me. "The rebels aren't the Blancos, Princess. They're barbaric. If they get their hands on you, they'll use you before torturing you. For weeks if not months. I will not risk you."

"I can fight," I hiss at him.

Damien moves fast, and before I can think to fend him off, he shoves me back against the wall, and pressing his body against mine, he growls, "Fight me off."

I try to squirm out of his hold, but Damien uses more strength than I'm used to, keeping me pinned. As my breaths speed up, he moves a hand between my legs and cups me hard.

With his face an inch from mine, he growls, "I can take you right here, and you won't be able to stop me. How will you stop a whole group of savages?"

My body relaxes in his hold, and then I whisper, "I'll have you." I let out a breath, my eyes not leaving his. "You'll never let anything happen to me."

Damien slackens his grip, and then his mouth crashes against mine. The kiss is bruising and controlling, a punishment for arguing with him. He ravages my lips and tongue until they're tingling from all the friction before his mouth moves down my throat.

Breathless, I say, "I'll always be safest at your side. Don't leave me behind."

Damien grabs hold of my thighs and lifts me against his body. The moment I wrap my legs around him, he carries me back to our bedroom. He kicks the door shut behind us and walks us to the bed, where he drops me.

My heartbeat speeds up as he rips my boots and pants off, and I try to prepare myself for his intensity. Damien doesn't even bother taking off his clothes. He just unbuckles his belt and unzips his pants. After freeing his cock, he yanks my legs apart and enters me hard.

He's relentless as he takes me, and it doesn't take long before we're both breathless from our orgasms seizing our bodies.

My body's still convulsing when Damien wraps his hand around my neck and yanks my face closer to his. "I will not put you in a position where another man can take what's mine. You will not be present during negotiations with the rebels. Don't fight me on this."

I will. I'll find a way to convince him. Maybe not this moment but definitely before the next run.

Damien must see the defiance on my face because his features turn to granite as he bites out, "Your life is not your own anymore, Princess. You belong to me, and it's time you realize that. When I say no, it's not negotiable."

"Everything's negotiable," I murmur. "Everything but death."

Damien's eyes narrow on mine before he pulls out of me. I watch him walk to the bathroom, his tense posture telling me he's raging mad.

Instead of giving him time to calm down, I go after him. "I'm not some fragile princess, Damien. I can handle a gun just as well as you. Not every fight will result in hand-to-hand combat. I'll be armed to the teeth during the runs."

He gives me a sideways glance as he braces his hands on the counter by the sink.

I move closer and place my hand on his back, leaning into him. "I'll show you when we attack the Blancos. Let me prove to you I can hold my own."

Damien stares long and hard at me before he grumbles, "If you do a single thing wrong, this discussion is over, and you will do as I say."

At least he's giving me a chance. I nod as I agree, "That's all I ask. Just give me a chance."

He lifts his hand, and wrapping it around the back of my neck, he pulls me against his body. I feel his breath in my hair before his lips skim over my ear and jaw. "I won't lose you," he whispers.

"You won't," I assure him.

DAMIEN

Somehow Alexei managed to get plans of the Blanco's villa. After his six men arrived, all Russian of course, we gather around the dining room table, studying the best way to attack.

"We're ten people. We should split into two groups. One attacks from the front while the other breaches from behind," Alexei says, gesturing on the map.

"I'll take the back," I say. "With Winter and three men. We can use this entrance to gain entry to the house."

"Then Demitri and I will attack from the front. We need to move fast. We can't risk using explosives." He glances around the room. "Everyone knows how to pick a lock?" He's met with a chorus of grunts, then Alexei says, "Check your weapons before we head out." He glances between Winter and me as we check our Heckler and Kochs. "You're sure she can shoot?"

Winter's been in a fighting mood since yesterday, and before she can say something to Alexei, I take hold of the back of her neck.

"Yes," I mutter. "She's good."

I notice how every man's eyes lock on Winter, and I quickly pull her against my side. "Keep your eyes off my wife."

They instantly look everywhere but at her, and then she fucking chuckles.

God, help me with this woman.

"Time to hunt," Alexei says, a smile tugging at his mouth. "Let's go."

We all file out of the dining room, and Winter breaks free from me. I follow her to the kitchen and watch as she hugs Dana goodbye.

When I see the worry on the housekeeper's face, I say, "I'll bring her back. Alive."

Dana nods at me. "Please. She's all I have."

They hug one more time before Winter returns to my side, and then we walk out of the house toward the private jet. It will take us three hours to get to Italy with our plane, so at least it's a short trip.

Once we board, I pull Winter to the back and away from the other men. I push her down in the seat in the corner and sit down next to her.

"You're possessive," she mutters.

"Get used to it," I grumble as I strap her in. I put on my own seat belt, then take hold of her hand and weave my fingers through hers.

She leans closer to me, and I tilt my head as she whispers. "I like it. If we were alone on the plane, I'd get on my knees to show you how much."

Slowly, I turn my face to hers until our eyes meet. Winter reaches over the armrest with her other hand and presses her palm against my cock. She squeezes me as a tempting smile tugs at her mouth.

I grab hold of her hand and push down harder as I grumble, "Don't start something you can't finish."

With a seductive chuckle, she pulls back and settles into her chair.

"My fearless love," I murmur, the corner of my mouth curving up.

She leans closer again and presses a kiss to my lips. "Always remember that."

Shaking my head, I tighten my hold on her hand, and as we begin to take off, silence descends over the cabin.

When we near Italy, I murmur, "Never leave my side."

Winter lets out a huff. "I know."

I turn my eyes to hers. "Not even to go to the restroom. I mean it."

She narrows her gaze on me. "You expect me to tell you every time I need to pee?"

"Yes," I grumble. "The Cotroni's might be allies, but it doesn't mean I trust them."

"Is there anyone you trust with my safety?" she asks.

"There was," I mutter, but stop myself in time from bringing up Cillian. Instead, I say, "My brother and Alexei. That's it. No one else gets near you."

When the plane starts its descent, I murmur, "Wait for the other men to leave first. We'll exit last."

"Okay."

I let go of Winter's hand and pull my gun from behind my back. I check the clip and glancing at her, I instruct, "Check your weapon." I wait until she's ready, and rising to my feet, I pull her up. "Behind me."

God, I should've left her at home.

Chapter 22

WINTER

The air is loaded with tension as we descend the plane. Damien's on guard, and it makes me scan our surroundings vigilantly as I follow him to an armored SUV.

He opens the door and shoves me inside. When he climbs in behind me, I shoot him a scowl. "You don't have to push me around."

"Don't start," he growls at me, his eyes constantly searching our surroundings for any threat.

Alexei and Demitri climb into the front, and as soon as Alexei starts the engine and pulls away, Damien relaxes a little.

His jaw is still clenched, though. I reach up and brush my fingers over his jaw, and it has him leaning into my palm. He places his hand over the back of mine, and our eyes meet.

Damien stares at me for a moment, and then he yanks me closer to him. His arms wrap tightly around me, and I feel his harsh breaths against my neck.

"I'm going to be okay," I try to reassure him.

"I shouldn't have brought you," he growls. "God, what was I thinking?"

I wrap my arms around his neck and press my mouth to his ear. "You've seen what I can do. Don't doubt me now. I'll hold my own as good as any man."

He nods as he takes a deep breath. "Just don't leave my side. No matter what happens."

"I won't. I'll stick to you like glue," I assure him.

He pulls a little back, and his eyes dart over my face, then he whispers, "Ya lyublyu tebya."

I shake my head, not understanding a word. Still, it's damn hot hearing him speak Russian.

He presses a kiss to my mouth then breathes against my lips, "I love you."

I smile against him as the words settle warmly in my heart. "I love you, too."

Damien kisses me as if he's trying to taste the words on my tongue until Alexei grumbles, "Come on. Not in the back seat. It's all I see when I look in the rearview mirror."

I let out a chuckle as Damien pulls away from me until I see the bewildered look in his eyes.

"What's wrong?" I ask.

"Nothing." The word is short, and it feels as if it instantly creates a distance between us.

I've never seen Damien like this, and worry begins to spin a web around my heart.

Does he regret telling me he loves me?

I have to keep the question to myself while we drive to the Cotroni's villa. When Alexei steers us onto the safety of the Cotroni's grounds with the other men following behind us, Damien seems to relax a little bit.

He opens the door and pulls me out of the car. The second I'm out, he tugs me right against his side, his eyes scanning everywhere again.

Alexei takes the lead with Demitri a step behind him, and then we follow with the other men bringing up the rear.

The front door opens, and Luca smiles welcoming at us. "Good to see you had a safe trip. Come in," The head of the Mafia greets us.

Luca shakes the men's hand then turns to me, and it instantly makes Damien tense up. His grip on my hand tightens into a crushing hold as Luca takes hold of my shoulders, kissing me on both my cheeks.

"Sorry for your losses, mi cara."

"Thank you," I murmur, flexing my fingers in Damien's hold so he'll ease up.

When we step into the villa, I tug at Damien's hand, whispering, "You're hurting me."

His grip on me loosens slightly as we follow Luca to a room where the weapons are waiting for us.

Alexei and Demitri immediately begin to inspect our shipment. Damien tugs me closer to a crate, and it has me saying, "You can let go. I won't disappear."

He lets out a low growl as his hand finally frees mine. I give him a questioning look, and stepping closer so only he will hear me, I ask, "What's going on with you?"

Damien shoots me a dark glare before taking a submachine gun from the crate. He inspects it, checking the clip.

Letting out a sigh, I pick up a Coharie CA-415 with a shortened barrel. It's the American-made version of the Heckler & Koch HK416, so I think I'll be most comfortable using it.

"A gift," Luca says, gesturing to a pile of backpacks. "To take extra ammunition. My scout reports no out-of-the-ordinary activity at Blanco's villa, but one can never be too prepared. Right?"

"Right," Alexei chuckles. "Thank you."

I walk away from Damien and grab two bags. When I turn around, he's right behind me, a murderous expression tightening his features.

"This is becoming absurd," I mutter as I shove a bag against his chest. I take my own and begin to load my selection of weapons and ammo while my temper flares to life.

DAMIEN

As soon as we have what we'll need for the attack, I shrug the backpack over my shoulder and grab hold of Winter. I pull her behind me as I walk to Luca.

"Where's the restroom?" I ask him.

"Down the hall, first door on the right."

I nod at him as I leave the group and drag Winter to the restroom. I shove her inside, and as soon as I shut the door behind us, she snaps, "What the hell, Damien?"

I try to breathe through the fear clawing at my heart. The emotion is foreign and overwhelming.

What was I thinking? God. If something happens to her, I'll never forgive myself.

Winter inches closer to me, and I shake my head. She reaches up and framing my jaw with her palms, she says, "Talk to me. What's going on?"

"I can't focus with you here," I admit the words I never thought would cross my lips. It's the one thing I could always pride myself on. Having focus. Going in, getting the job done, and getting out.

Understanding settles in her eyes. "Remember the laser game?"

I nod.

"No one shot me."

"That was a fucking game," I growl.

"At the hanger. That wasn't a game. I killed three men and didn't get myself shot, and I was beside myself. I'm focused now. You need to believe in my abilities, Damien."

My eyes dart over the woman who's reduced me to a worrying mess.

She's small.

She's fast.

Winter can handle a gun.

She doesn't miss a target.

My breaths slow down, and the worry retreats slightly.

Taking hold of Winter, I pull her against my chest and hold her tightly. "I can't lose you."

"You won't," she murmurs.

I pull back and stare down at her.

So this is love? Worrying every second of every day that I might lose her? Threatening every man that dares to look at her? Fighting her into submission? Fearing the day I won't be there to protect her?

"I don't want to love you so much," I admit.

Winter frowns at me.

"It's driving me insane."

She lifts herself on her toes and presses a tender kiss to my mouth.

"That's not helping at all," I grumble at her.

She lets out a soft burst of laughter as she presses another kiss to my lips, then she murmurs, "Isn't that what obsession is? It drives us insane for each other, so we're willing to do the unthinkable for the other person."

I lift my hand to her face and brush my fingers over her soft skin. "I'll burn the world down for you if that's what it takes to keep you safe."

A beautiful smile lifts her lips. "I'm obsessed with you too, Damien."

"Don't leave my side again. I can't think straight if you're not next to me."

She nods quickly. "I won't. I promise."

I stare deep into her eyes, and seeing the love she feels for me, calms the storm in my chest.

"Are you ready?" Winter asks.

I nod and kiss her one more time before we leave the restroom.

We return to the group, and Demitri comes to stand next to me. "Should I worry?"

I shake my head as I meet my brother's eyes. "I'm ready."

Demitri hands us earpieces. "So we can communicate."

We each take one and place it in our ears, and then we shake Luca's hand. As we leave, he mutters, "Good luck."

With our weapons, we take two SUVs, splitting into groups. I climb in behind the steering wheel and start the engine. As I follow after Demitri, Winter murmurs, "This is it." Excitement flushes her cheeks. "I get to watch them all die."

I place my hand on her thigh and give it a squeeze before returning it to the steering wheel.

Under the cover of darkness, we reach the road where we have to split up.

Demitri's voice comes over the earpiece, "Let one of the men stay with the car and keep a lookout for reinforcements or the police. Be safe."

"You too," I murmur, and then I turn up the road that will take us to the back of the villa.

I park the car a couple of meters from the house, and getting out, I scan the area for any kind of threat. I sling the submachine gun over my shoulder and keep the Heckler and Koch in my hand as I walk around the car. Winter shrugs on her backpack, also holding her gun ready for use.

"Sergei, stay with the car," I order.

He nods and climbs in behind the steering wheel.

I take a deep breath, and then I lead my group toward the wall. I use one of the men to hoist myself up the wall and then reach down for Winter. Her fingers fold around mine, and I pull her quickly up. I wait for her to climb over and then jump after her. We land in crouching positions and wait for the other two to join us.

"Sensors," Yuri whispers, gesturing to the beams scattered over the yard.

"We have to crawl," I mutter.

It takes longer than I had hoped it would as we slowly inch our way toward the back of the villa. Lights shine from rooms, and it gives us a clear view of the men guarding the house.

"Are you ready?" Demitri asks.

"Not yet," I breathe. "Two minutes."

When we pass under the last beam, I whisper, "Ready."

"Breach!" Demitri instructs, and the four of us jump to our feet, and with exact precision, we attack.

As a guard turns in our direction, I open fire, and then all hell breaks loose at the front of the house as Demitri and Alexei enter with their men.

Winter stays by my side, and with every step I take, she matches it. Yuri takes out a guard on the balcony while Winter gets one as he comes rushing out of the house.

"Good," I murmur as I set my sights on another guard, taking him down with a shot to the head.

"Four down," I notify Demitri. Their gunfire sounds through the house as we enter through a sliding door.

"Blyad'," Alexei curses. "I got the son. He pissed himself."

"Vince?" Winter asks as we move through a living room.

"Yes."

He must've left St. Monarch's after the assassination of Winter's family.

"Don't kill Antonio. He's mine," she growls.

As we turn down a hallway, we're met with more guards, but not the amount we anticipated. Seems the Blancos weren't expecting Winter to retaliate but to go into hiding again.

We open fire, and I take them down as quickly as I can. My heart pounds in my chest every time a gun is raised in Winter's direction.

Suddenly, Antonio Blanco comes out of a room, holding a woman as a shield. Winter immediately starts shooting. The woman takes four bullets before Antonio shoves her toward us, making a run down some stairs.

"Coward," I hiss as we reach the woman.

She's gasping for air, but then Winter crouches next to her, whispering darkly, "A mother for a mother." Winter rises to her feet then puts a bullet in the woman's head.

"Moving to a lower level," I advise Demitri.

"Coming your way," he replies.

Cautiously, I descend the stairs, not knowing what we'll be met with.

Chapter 23

WINTER

"Blyad'," Damien hisses when he catches sight of something I can't see yet. He freezes, then says, "Stay here, Winter."

Like hell I am!

Damien moves forward, his gun trained on someone, while shaking his head.

Refusing to miss my one chance at killing Antonio, I move forward, and then the air is ripped from my lungs.

"Cillian," I gasp.

Antonio holds him as a shield, a gun trained against Cillian's head.

My breathing speeds up at seeing the man I've mourned, still alive, albeit barely. It's clear they've tortured him, his left eye swollen shut and his hands covered in blood.

He's in bad shape, and without giving it another thought, I lift my gun.

"I will kill him," Antonio threatens, and then I pull the trigger just as Cillian yanks free, falling to his hands and knees. My bullet hits Antonio between the eyes, and I keep firing as I move closer, in a hurry to get Cillian.

Antonio stumbles backward before he slumps to the ground. I rush to Cillian, where he's trying to push himself up. Every breath he takes sends a wave of pain over his face as I kneel before him. Then he whispers, "Poppet." Cillian collapses against me.

"My God," I sob as I wrap my arms around him. "My God." Absolute joy floods me, making my head spin as I try to process it. "Cillian."

"All the training paid off," he chuckles, a whistling sound escaping him.

"I thought you died," I cry as I hug him tighter. "We couldn't find your body."

"I woke up here," he gasps through pain, and I ease my hold on him.

"We need to move." Damien crouches on Cillian's side and pulls Cillian's arm around his neck as he takes hold of him. I do the same, and then we help Cillian stand.

Still in shock, I try to take as much of Cillian's weight as I can.

"Who's this?" Alexei asks as he comes down the stairs.

"God, Poppet," Cillian breathes at the sight of Alexei Koslov.

"He's my family," I say, tightening my hold around Cillian's back.

Alexei moves closer. "You're too small, little Winter. Move."

I let Alexei take my place, and then we can move faster as we make our way out of the basement. I keep my body positioned in front of Cillian, my gun raised and ready to fire.

I won't lose him a second time.

"Sergei, bring the car around the front," Damien instructs.

We make our way through the bodies of the guards Alexei and his group took down, and then I see Vince lying face down, his back riddled with bullets.

Burn in hell with your family, bastard.

Leaving the mansion, we move quickly to get to the cars. It's a struggle getting Cillian over the wall, and his pain-filled breaths rip at my heart.

When we finally reach the first SUV, I climb in the back with Cillian. Damien gets in next to me while Alexei takes the driver's side and Demitri the passenger side.

The other men pile into the other SUV, and then we leave for the private airfield.

I keep staring at Cillian, still not able to believe he's alive. My eyes scan over his body and seeing his bruises, I wish I could kill the Blancos again. I shudder as I begin to see more wounds. He's missing an earlobe. Broken nose. Old and new bruises coloring his face and neck.

"We'll take care of you as soon as we're home," I say, my voice hoarse. "Can you hold out a couple of hours?"

"Walk in the park after the past four days," he mumbles.

I watch as he fights to remain conscious, his eyes glued to mine. "My Poppet."

My lips tremble as I try to smile at him. "My Cillian."

Alexei parks by the private jet, and then he helps Damien get Cillian into the plane. I take the seat next to Cillian and strap him in. His head lolls to the side, his eyes locking on me again.

"We're going home," I murmur as I put on my own seat belt.

Damien takes a seat across from me, his eyes darting between Cillian and me.

When we take off, Cillian whispers, "Home."

I watch as his eyes drift shut, then Demitri says, "That's good. Let him sleep." As soon as we reach altitude, Demitri goes to get a first aid kit then tells me, "Move to another chair."

I get up and take the seat next to Damien and across from Cillian. Demitri opens the box and takes out an injection which has me asking, "What's that?"

"It will help keep him sedated while we check how badly he got hurt."

As soon as he administers the injection, Demitri begins to unbutton Cillian's shirt. There's a bandage around him, but blood has already seeped through and dried to black.

"Help me, Winter," Demitri instructs, and I move off the seat. "Hold him so I can take this bandage off.

I pull Cillian to me and let his head rest against my stomach while Demitri goes to work. After a minute or so, Demitri mutters, "Looks like he has an infection. We'll need to get antibiotics in him."

"We have supplies at home," I answer. "We made sure to have everything needed to treat a gunshot after I got shot."

"Good," Damien murmurs.

"You can lean him back," Demitri says, and as I carefully position Cillian's head against the seat, I glance down at the gunshot wound he took to the chest. It's swollen and red around the bullet hole, and there's a dark bruise spreading over the side of his chest.

Demitri covers the wound with a clean dressing. "As soon as we get home, get me the antibiotics."

"Okay," I murmur, my eyes scanning over Cillian in disbelief.

Damien takes hold of my hand and pulls me to the restroom. Just like the time when I thought Cillian was dead, Damien washes the blood off my hands and gently dries them.

"Thank you," I murmur, and then it sinks in, knocking the breath from my lungs. "Cillian's alive," I gasp as the first tear of absolute joy falls.

DAMIEN

I pull Winter into my arms and press a kiss to her hair. "I'm happy for you, Princess."

I hold her while she struggles to regain control over her emotions, and when she finally looks up at me, I press a kiss to her lips.

"Let's take our seats. We'll land soon."

Getting back to the seats, Winter checks Cillian's seat belt before she sits down. I strap her in and then take hold of her hand, linking my fingers with hers.

Demitri puts the first aid kit away. After he washes his hands, he sits down next to Alexei and straps himself in.

Our eyes meet, and the corner of my mouth lifts as pride fills my chest.

As soon as the plane touches down, we get up, and Demitri helps me carry Cillian off the plane.

Winter runs ahead to the house, and then I hear her call out, "Dana! Dana!" The front door opens, and as Dana appears, Winter yells, "We have Cillian. He's alive."

Dana's hand goes to her mouth when her eyes land on us, and then she rushes back inside the house with Winter right behind her.

When we carry Cillian inside, Dana urgently says, "His room is across from Miss Winter's. She's gone to unlock it." She follows after us as we take Cillian upstairs.

Winter comes rushing out of his room, and when she sees us, she darts back inside. She pulls the bedding back before we carefully lay Cillian down.

"Dana," Demitri calls. "Help me get the clothes off so we can check all his wounds."

I walk to Winter and take hold of her arm. "Leave them to tend to him. I'm sure he wouldn't want you to see him naked."

Winter nods, and sparing Cillian a last glance, she follows me out of the room. As soon as we step into the hallway, Winter wraps her arms around my waist.

"God, Damien, he's alive. We left him behind for them to torture."

Holding her to me, I say, "We didn't know. It looked like he died."

"I should've checked," she blames herself.

Placing a finger under her chin, I nudge her face up, and when our eyes lock, I say, "No, you had no choice. I pulled you away, and there was no way I was endangering your life a second longer. I'd do it again."

Winter pulls out of my hold. "Would you have left him there if you had known he was alive?"

"Of course not," I mutter.

"Where's Demitri?" Alexei asks.

I gesture at the closed door. "In there with Cillian."

Alexei turns his gaze to Winter. "Where are the antibiotics?"

"Oh, in the kitchen." Winter rushes away to go get it.

"She did well today," Alexei mutters.

"She did."

"Will you let her go on runs with you?"

I stare down the hallway before bringing my gaze to Alexei's. "Not if I can help it."

"She'll fight you."

"I know," I mutter. Winter proved herself today. She was caught off guard by Cillian being there, but still, she kept her calm and killed Antonio Blanco. Not once did she hesitate.

"Maybe if Cillian recovers, you'll allow it," Alexei mentions.

I narrow my gaze on him. "Why are you pushing this?"

"She'll resent you if you try to keep her out of the business."

I let out a breath of air. "We'll see what happens."

Winter comes back, carrying a first aid kit which she hands to Alexei. "Everything's in here."

Alexei takes it into the room, and then I say, "Let's go gather the weapons and put them away."

Together we leave the house and reaching the plane, the other men have already off-loaded everything. We inspect the weapons before carrying them to the barn. There's a trap door, and opening it, we descend into the Hemsley's armory.

We stack all the machine guns and extra handguns before I close the trap door and lock it.

Keeping our personal weapons with us, we head back to the house.

The extra men Alexei organized go to the kitchen to help themselves to food while Winter and I head up the stairs to Cillian's room.

"Let me check," I murmur as I push the door open. Seeing Cillian's covered from the waist down, I pull Winter into the room.

"How's he doing?" she asks.

"He'll be out of it for a few days. He needs to rest and heal from the infection. That's my biggest worry," Demitri says. "Dana will be able to care for him."

My eyes lock with my brother's. "You're leaving?"

He nods. "The job's done here. We need to get back to LA."

"When are you heading back?" I ask.

"Tomorrow morning."

"Thank you for all the help," Winter murmurs as she walks to Cillian's side. She takes the cloth from Demitri's hand. "I'll continue to wash him."

Demitri and I step out into the hallway while the women clean Cillian.

"You'll be okay?" Demitri asks.

"I will," I assure him. Seeing the concern in his eyes, I say, "I have to do this. The sooner, the better."

"Alexei expects his fifty percent paid on time. Don't mess it up."

"I won't."

Demitri gives my shoulder a squeeze before he leaves. I lean my shoulder against the doorjamb and watch as Winter carefully washes Cillian's neck.

My gaze locks on Cillian. I have no idea how he'll react when he finds out I took Winter as my wife and Alexei took half the business.

He'll probably lose his shit.

Chapter 24

WINTER

Once Cillian's clean, the bruises are prominent, and it tells a stark tale of how much he must've suffered.

I sit down on a chair while Dana sits down on the side of the bed. She brushes her fingers through Cillian's hair, tears silently spiraling over her cheeks.

"My love," she whispers. "I should've known they wouldn't be able to kill you." Leaning over him, she presses a soft kiss to his lips. "Thank you for coming back to us."

It's the first time I see Dana interact in such a loving way toward Cillian.

"Why did you hide your relationship?"

Dana swallows hard then gives me a trembling smile. "Your father would've worried. Cillian's attention needed to be focused on you."

It was. He never left my side at the expense of his own happiness.

Now that I've experienced my own love with Damien, I can only imagine how hard it must've been for Cillian and Dana.

"I'm sorry," I murmur.

Instantly Dana shakes her head. "We love you like our own, Miss Winter. It was our choice."

My gaze turns to Cillian, and a burst of happiness explodes inside me.

He's home.

I didn't lose everyone.

Emotion wells in my chest, but I swallow it down and clear my throat.

The time for crying has passed. Now it's time to celebrate the wins we've had.

My lips curve up at the thought of the Blancos being wiped out. I'm disappointed at how fast it happened. There was no time to savor the kills.

But they are dead. They've paid with their own lives for the family they've taken from me.

My enemies now know what I'm capable of. Word will spread of my marriage to Damien. People will know of my alliance with Alexei and Demitri.

I stare at Cillian and Dana. The couple who have sacrificed so much for me.

It's my turn to keep them safe.

"You and Cillian can now enjoy your relationship," I murmur. Dana's eyes dart to mine. "I'll take care of you. I don't want you to worry about me any longer. Damien will take over as the head of the family, and together we will keep you safe."

Dana reaches her hand to me, and I don't hesitate to take hold of it.

"Thank you, Miss Winter." Dana gets up and gives Cillian a last glance before she says, "I'll prepare something to eat. The men must be hungry."

As the sun begins to rise, I move from the chair to the bed and sitting down, I carefully take Cillian's hand in my own.

My eyes drink in his features. "Rest and get better. Your time of protecting me is over." I lean forward and press a kiss to his forehead. "It's my turn to look after you."

Emotion wells in my chest, and I allow a tear to fall.

"Thank you for being my father, my mother, my mentor, my best friend. Thank you for fighting so hard to get back to me."

Cillian lets out a sharp breath, and then his eyes drift open. I smile as he focuses on my face.

"Poppet," he breathes.

"Hi," I grin happily at him. "How do you feel?"

"A little worse for wear," he mumbles.

"Demitri gave you some antibiotics and cleaned your wounds. We'll have you back on your feet in no time."

A lopsided grin forms around his lips, and I struggle not to cry from the joy of seeing it again. "I missed that smile so much," I admit.

His eyes rest on me with endless love. "I didn't tell them, poppet."

"Didn't tell them what?"

"Where you were. Where the island is," he says, already short of breath from the strain it's taking to talk.

Cillian suffered to keep me safe.

"I love you so much, Cillian," is all I can think to say as I press another kiss to his forehead. "Rest. I'll take care of you from now on."

"My poppet," he breathes before his eyes drift closed.

I sit with Cillian until Dana comes back. "He woke for a moment," I tell her. "He was lucid."

"I'll stay with him. Go eat, Miss Winter."

I nod my head, and getting up from the bed, I softly leave the room as Dana takes my place to keep vigil over Cillian.

I find the men in the dining room, filling their stomachs with the breakfast Dana prepared. I sit down on Damien's right.

"Cillian woke," I inform them as I help myself to some pancakes and eggs.

"Good," Alexei mutters. "I'm glad you got your friend back."

I can't stop smiling as I enjoy breakfast with my new family.

"Alexei and Demitri are leaving today," Damien says as I take a bite of the pancakes.

My eyes dart to the two men as I chew and swallow, then I ask, "So soon? You can't stay a little longer?"

Alexei shakes his head. "Business waits for no one."

My shoulders sag a bit. "Thank you for helping me."

"That's what family is for," Demitri murmurs.

I meet my brother-in-law's eyes for a long moment. We didn't have any time to get to know each other. "You'll come to visit when you can?"

Demitri nods. "Not often, though." His gaze moves to Damien's. "You could always travel to LA."

"We have to sell the diamonds," Alexei interrupts. "The buyer is in New York. We could meet you there."

Damien and I both nod at the news.

"That way, you'll take your rightful place as diamond smugglers in the Ruin," Alexei adds.

As Mr. and Mrs. Vetrov, our enemies will know we're unkillable and merciless. Hopefully, our name alone will be enough to prevent another blood bath.

DAMIEN

With Winter next to me, we see Alexei and Demitri off.

I hug Alexei before embracing my brother.

"Keep safe," Demitri murmurs.

"You too."

He pulls back, and with his hands on my shoulders, our gazes lock. "You've done well. I'm proud of you."

The corner of my mouth curves up at hearing my brother's praise.

As they board the plane, Winter takes hold of my hand, snuggling against my side.

"We'll be okay without them, right?" she asks.

I pull my hand free from hers and wrap my arm around her shoulders. Pressing a kiss to her temple, my voice is low and filled with strength as I say, "We'll be okay."

Winter lifts her face to mine, her mouth curving into a smile. "I love you, my husband."

Lifting an eyebrow, I steer her toward the house. "We have to tell Cillian we're married." A grimace forms on her face, and I let out a chuckle. "Let me handle it."

"Good, when I'm done nursing Cillian back to health, I can nurse you when he's done beating you up," she teases me.

"I'd like to see him try." I let out a chuckle as we step into the house – our home.

"I'm going to check on Cillian," Winter says. "What are you going to do?"

"Take care of business."

Winter turns her face up to me, and I press a kiss to her mouth.

"I'll help with the business once Cillian has recovered."

"Don't worry. I'll take care of everything."

I watch her walk up the stairs then leave the house to check on the guards stationed around the island. I need to get to know every single one of them. It takes me a couple of hours as I walk around the grounds, familiarizing myself with where everything is.

When I reach the men guarding the piers, I ask, "Names and how long have you worked here?"

"Phil. Eleven years," the first and oldest of the three answers.

My gaze snaps to the second man. "Jasper. Seven years."

When my eyes lock on the last man, he gives me a condescending look. "Petro. Five years."

"Petro," I grumble, taking a threatening step toward him. "Do we have a problem?"

"Not at all," he mutters while smirking as if he knows something I'm not aware of.

I take another step closer to him and stare him down until he glances away. "You're welcome to leave," I murmur darkly. "In a body bag." His eyes snap back to mine, and I see a glimmer of fear. "I'm not Patrick Hemsley or Cillian. Don't fuck with me."

Petro nods and wisely backs a step away from me. "Yes, Sir."

I make my way back to the house, and reaching Cillian's room, I murmur, "Winter, come here."

She lets go of Cillian's hand, and when she steps out into the hallway, I shut the door, so Dana won't hear us talk.

Winter gives me a questioning look, then asks, "What's wrong?"

"I went to check on the guards, and one gave me attitude." The more I think about the incident, the more I wish I had just killed him. I won't tolerate insubordination. "How well do you know them?"

"Well enough. Which one do you have a problem with?"

"Petro. He's stationed by the piers."

I watch as Winter's eyes widen, then she quickly says, "I'll take care of him. Don't worry about it."

Tilting my head, my heartbeat begins to speed up. My voice is a low warning as I ask, "Is there something I should know?" Winter steps closer to me and places her hand on my arm as if she's trying to placate me. My expression hardens. "Don't dare lie to me. Have you fucked him?"

"It was before you –"

I walk away before she can finish the sentence and rush out of the house in the direction of the piers. Anger burns through my veins. Every time I start to think about that fucker with my wife, even if it was before she married me, unreasonable rage engulfs me.

"Damien!" I hear Winter call behind me.

Halfway there, I pull my gun from behind my back, and my finger hovers over the trigger. With every step I take, the rage burns hotter, like an inferno incinerating all logic, until my vision tunnels on the three men ahead of me.

"Damien, wait!" Winter catches up to me and grabs hold of my arm.

I shrug her off, and one dark glare from me is enough for her to stop walking.

Jasper notices me first and quickly says something to the other two. As Petro's head snaps in my direction, I raise the gun, and I don't stop walking until the barrel is pressed against his skull.

"You fucked my wife?"

He just stares at me as fear pales his face.

Without a second thought, I pull the trigger, then I turn my gaze to Phil. "Has anyone else on this island fucked her?"

"No, Sir," he answers immediately.

"Dispose of the body," I growl the order.

"Yes, Sir."

I walk back to where Winter's standing, her eyes wide on me. Stopping right in front of her, my voice is low with anger, "I better be the only man alive who's fucked you."

"You are," she breathes.

It's only then the rage begins to lose its potency, and I breathe through the rest of the anger until I'm in control of my emotions.

"You're the only one I love. I haven't loved before you," Winter says, a pleading look on her face.

The words help calm me, and I reach for her neck, wrapping my fingers around her throat. I pull her to me, and Winter tilts her head back to keep eye contact with me.

Her hands find my sides, and she grips hold of my shirt. "There's only you, Damien."

Leaning down, I claim her mouth, kissing her until she's gasping against my lips and my lungs burn for air.

Chapter 25

WINTER

I must've fallen asleep on the chair next to Cillian's bed because I'm woken by Damien as he lifts me to his chest.

He carries me to our bed and lays me down. Without a word, he pulls my shirt over my head. His fingers curl into the waistband of my sweatpants, and he tugs the fabric off, along with my panties.

I watch as he throws the clothes in the laundry basket before taking off his own. He turns off the lights then comes to climb into bed. When his hand grips hold of my hip, I snuggle closer until I'm pressed against his chest.

Silence fills the room. I rest my hand on his bare skin and press a kiss to his throat.

"The first time I saw you, I never could've imagined this would be our future," I murmur.

"A lot has happened in five weeks."

"Yeah, I'm sure you never thought you'd love me," I tease him, not wanting the incident from this afternoon to affect our relationship. Honestly, I haven't thought about Petro or Damien finding out. It was the last thing on my mind.

"It was hard pushing my feelings for you aside," he admits.

I lift my head and meet his eyes. "Do you regret not being auctioned off to Carson?"

Damien brings his hand to my face and draws a line from my temple to my lips. "At first, I was angry, but then I was made an offer I couldn't resist."

"Marrying me?" Keeping my palm flat on his skin, I move my hand down until I reach his cock. I wrap my fingers around his length and begin to slowly stroke him.

Damien nods as he rolls me onto my back. "Claiming you." He positions himself between my legs and begins to rub his hardness against my clit. Lowering his head, his teeth tug at my bottom lip, and then he leaves a trail of kisses and bites down my throat before coming back to my mouth.

I feel his hand between us, his knuckles brushing over my clit, as he positions his cock by my opening. He thrusts inside me, and I gasp against his lips. I expect him to take me hard, but instead, he keeps still as he begins to deepen the kiss.

It's different from the ones before. It feels as if Damien's making love to my mouth, his tongue caressing me with strong strokes, and his lips kneading mine until I moan against him.

He pulls out of me before slowly entering me, filling me with every inch of him. When he keeps the pace agonizingly slow, I whimper into his mouth.

Damien breaks the kiss, and lifting his head, he locks eyes with me.

He pulls out again, and this time when he slowly enters me, he asks, "Do you feel me?"

"Every inch," I breathe.

The moment becomes loaded with intensity as he keeps my gaze imprisoned. Emotion begins to build in my chest as he pushes inside me again.

Damien's making love to me. For the first time.

My breaths begin to rush over my lips, and overwhelmed by the realization, I blink fast to keep the tears back.

He pushes his arm under my body and gripping me tightly to him, his mouth finds mine again. He sweeps me away from this world to a place where only we exist.

I fall so hard, so unbelievably fast, from how passionately he's kissing me. I savor every stroke as he fills me. I inhale his breaths. My arms wrap tightly around his broad back, and I cling to the man who's become my life.

"You own me," I whimper, and it's all it takes for Damien to lose control.

He begins to drive into me, harder and faster with every thrust until my body bows against his. Pleasure rips through me like a devasting tornado.

Panting against his mouth, I breathe in his growl as he finds his own release. His muscled body jerks against mine, and then I take his weight as he collapses on top of me.

For a long moment, our breathing is all that fills the air as we cling to each other.

Damien is the first to move, lifting his head so he can look at me. Our eyes meet, and then he murmurs, "Slava ne mogut apisat' mayu lyubof' k tebe."

My lips curve up at hearing the Russian words. "What does it mean?"

"Words can't describe my love for you."

Lifting my head, I press a tender kiss to his mouth.

DAMIEN

Cillian's been sleeping on and off for the past three days, but when he's finally awake enough to sit up in bed, I walk into the room to check on him.

Before I can ask how he's feeling, Cillian gestures to Winter's left hand. "What the fuck is that on her finger?"

"Cillian," Winter begins, but I shake my head at her to keep quiet as I step closer to the bed.

"It's my ring. Winter's my wife."

Cillian stares at me, and I watch as anger tightens his features. "You fucking forced her into a marriage?"

"It was an alliance. No one forced Winter to do anything she didn't agree to."

"She lost her family. She thought she lost me. Four fucking days and you take over," Cillian begins to rage at me.

"She had a choice," I bite the words out.

"What choice?" he growls. "She's a young woman up against the Vetrovs and Koslovs. What fucking choice did that leave her?"

I take a calming breath, knowing I can't lose my temper.

"I love him," Winter interrupts, her voice soft. Cillian's gaze snaps to her, and she repeats, "I love, Damien. It was my choice to marry him."

"How? You barely know him. A month at St. Monarch's while you were supposed to focus on your training. When did you have time to fall in love?"

Winter holds Cillian's gaze as she admits, "The moment I laid eyes on him."

"Come on, poppet," he scoffs. "Love at first sight? That's nothing but a fairytale."

"Not to me, it isn't," she begins to argue, and it makes the corner of my mouth lift. "Damien's everything I want in a man. You said it yourself when you told me stories of the Vetrovs. He's merciless, unkillable, with a devastating potency no one can escape. That's what I wanted, what I needed to survive in this world, and he was able to give it to me."

Even though Winter knew that about me, she never backed down.

Cillian turns his attention back to me. "And you? Was it only for the business?"

I shake my head. "It was for her fiery spirit."

I watch as the anger retreats from his face as my words sink in.

"I love her."

Cillian takes a deep breath, a twinge of pain on his face, then he leans back against the pillows. He's quiet for a moment before he says, "You can be glad I'm stuck in this bed, or it would be you and me in the barn."

Unable to keep a straight face, I begin to smile. "We'll wait until you're back on your feet."

His eyes move between Winter and me. "Christ, poppet. Only you would marry a Vetrov."

She lets out a chuckle. "You know me, I always wanted the best."

He pins me with a look of warning. "Don't hurt her."

"I won't."

"What about the business?" Cillian asks.

God, here we go for round two.

Squaring my shoulders, I say, "Alexei gets fifty percent."

Cillian blinks at me, then he mutters, "Say that again."

"Alexei will arrange the buyers."

Cillian's eyes dart between Winter and me. "Fifty percent?"

"For his protection and support, yes," I answer.

I'm surprised when Cillian doesn't burst a vein but instead thinks about it, then he mutters, "Christ. Four days and the Vetrovs and Koslovs take over. You people don't waste any time."

"Time is money," I shrug.

"Who will do the runs and negotiations with the rebels?"

"I will."

"*We* will," Winter interrupts.

My gaze snaps to hers. "We're not having that conversation now." I turn my attention back to Cillian. "I'll take care of the business with Alexei's help."

"Good luck trying to keep this one away from the business," he mutters.

Again the corner of my mouth lifts and considering the conversation over, I say, "Time for dinner."

When Dana moves to get up from where she's sitting on the side of the bed, Winter says, "Don't worry. I'll plate the food and bring it to you."

Before we leave the room, Cillian mutters, "She might love you, but you'll have to prove yourself to me."

"Of course," I chuckle as I take hold of Winter's hand.

Leaving the room, Winter's quiet until we reach the kitchen. I take a seat at the island and watch as she begins to plate the lamb and vegetables Dana prepared.

"I will go with you on the runs," she grumbles, giving me a glare.

"It's not safe," I state the obvious. "I won't be able to focus on the job with you there."

"Damien," she snaps, her hands stilling. "I did everything right during the attack on the Blancos. I can hold my own. Stop trying to keep me locked away on the island. I won't stand for it."

Seeing the fire in her eyes, I begin to grow hard. "I'll fuck you on this table. I don't care if Dana walks in on us."

She makes a disgruntled sound through her nose. "Don't change the subject."

Rising to my feet, I go to stand behind Winter. I wrap my arms around her and slip a hand between her legs. "You know it's a turn-on when you fight me." I press a kiss to the scar on her neck and then suck hard as I begin to rub her through the clothes. "Still, you defy me every chance you get." Moving my hand up, I slip it under the fabric, and then my middle finger brushes over her sensitive nerves.

"I will go with," she breathes as she braces her hands on the table and tilts her head back.

With my free hand, I grab hold of her hair as I begin to rub her harder, only skimming over her opening.

"Damien," she gasps as she begins to ride my hand. "Please take me with." Her hips move in sync with my hand. "Please. Please. Please."

My lips curve up into a satisfied smirk as I make her orgasm, and then I murmur in her ear, "You don't leave my side during a run."

"I won't," she breathlessly agrees.

I pull my hand free from her pants and bring my middle finger to her mouth. "Suck, Princess."

Her lips open for me, and then her tongue swirls around my finger as she tastes herself.

"Feed Dana and Cillian and get food in your stomach so I can take you to bed," I order as I take a seat at the island again.

Winter gives me an alluring smile as she continues to plate the food.

God, this woman. I wonder if she knows what power she holds over me?

Chapter 26

WINTER

Going in search of Damien, I find him in my father's office. A frown darkens his face as he stares at something on the laptop.

"What are you doing?" I ask as I move around the desk to see what he's looking at.

"Checking the designated airport and surrounding areas of Sierra Leone for the next run," he murmurs deep in thought.

I glance over the map, then ask, "When are we going?"

Damien glances at me, and I can see he's still not happy with me going on the run. "Three days from now. I've made contact with the rebels this morning."

"Your father always said there was something special about the diamonds in Sierra Leone," Cillian suddenly says as he comes in. "They have a special light and coloring." Cillian takes a seat, a flash of pain on his face from the movement. "We're leaving in three days?"

"We?" I ask as I straighten up. "You're in no shape to travel."

"I'm fine," he grumbles. "There's no way I'm letting you face the RUF without me there."

"RUF?" I ask.

"Radical Unified Front," Damien mutters. "It's what the rebels call themselves."

"Cillian, you're still recovering," I state. "Sit this one out. I'll have Damien, and we're taking five men with us."

"Sierra Leone is not like any country you've been to, poppet," Cillian says. "It's ravaged by war. Issa Gbao, the leader of the RUF, will kill first, then ask questions. You can't argue with him the way you argue with us. I'm going with. I can handle a weapon, and someone needs to keep you on a leash."

Damien lets out a chuckle, and it has me narrowing my eyes at him before leveling Cillian with a scowl. "Don't treat me like I'm a child," I bite out. "I've bled for this business. I'm the Blood Princess. This is my legacy, and I will not let you and Damien keep me from taking my rightful place."

Losing my temper, I stalk out of the office, knowing I'll say something I'll regret. I'm tired of being treated as a lessor.

I walk out of the house and keep going until I find myself nearing the family cemetery. My pace slows down until I stop in front of my father's grave.

The anger keeps simmering in my chest as my gaze drifts over my loved ones' final resting place.

"They think I'm weak." I fist my hands at my sides as I try to slow my breathing down.

"I don't think you're weak," Damien suddenly says behind me.

I swing around, directing a glare at him. "You make me feel weak. Cillian as well. Neither of you trust me."

Damien shakes his head as he closes the distance between us. When he reaches for my neck, I pull away. His eyes snap to mine, and then his hand shoots out, and before I can move, his fingers wrap around my throat, and he yanks me to him.

His dark eyes penetrate mine as he growls, "I don't think you're weak, Princess. I just don't want you anywhere near danger. It fucking puts the fear of God in me, and it's an emotion I'm not comfortable with at all."

"I can take care of myself. How many times must I prove myself to you?" I snap as I grab hold of his wrist. Damien's eyes narrow on me. "You'll never see me as an equal, will you?"

The thought stabs through my heart.

His expression turns to granite as his fingers flex around my throat. "I'm fucking trying, Winter. I agreed to you going with me. What more do you want?"

My breaths explode over my lips as I cry, "Your respect! Not just your love. Not only your controlling possessiveness. I just want you to respect me as the Blood Princess." It feels like this fight's been coming since we got married, and now I can't stop the words from spilling from me. "I'm not just your wife. I'm a Mafia princess… a queen, and I demand to be treated as one. I killed Antonio Blanco. I fought for the Hemsley legacy. My family lies behind me."

Damien lets go and takes a step away from me. His body is tense, and his stare deadly.

"I can't have your fear crippling me," I say as I take a step toward him. "You're the strongest man I know, Damien. I need that strength behind me. We're either a team or nothing."

His jaw clenches at my words, and for a long moment, he just stares at me. "Fine."

I begin to frown. "Fine, what?"

"We're a team," he mutters.

My frown deepens. I expected him to lash out at me. "You agree with me?" I ask to make sure.

"Yes."

"You're not going to fuck me into submission?"

The corner of his mouth lifts into a sexy smirk. "Tonight, you will pay for the way you spoke to me, but right now, we have work to do."

Surprised by his reaction, I ask, "You won't fight me on this again?"

He lets out a silent chuckle. "We'll fight again, but for this run, you win."

"I'll win every time," I mutter as I begin to walk past him.

Damien's arm falls around my shoulders, then he chuckles, "My little spitfire."

"I'm an inferno," I grumble, but I don't pull away from him and instead wrap my arm around his lower back.

DAMIEN

As the plane comes to a standstill, my eyes snap between Winter and Cillian. "Let me do the talking."

Getting up from the seats, I check Winter's bulletproof vest before checking my own. "Recheck your weapons," I mutter.

Holding the submachine gun against my stomach, with the barrel facing down, I walk to the exit, and opening the door, I descend the stairs. Winter's right behind me, with Cillian and the men bringing up the rear.

As I step onto Sierra Leone ground, I hear vehicles, and then three jeeps appear from the bushes surrounding the airfield.

Each vehicle holds five men, all armed to the teeth. I take a deep breath. "Don't bring the briefcase until I give the all-clear signal."

I wait for the jeeps to come to a stop in a cloud of dust before I walk toward them.

One of the rebels jumps off and walks toward me, a merciless gleam in his eyes. I meet his gaze, and when we stop a couple of feet from each other, his eyes sweep over me with disgust. "Vetrov?" he spits my name out.

"Gbao," I mutter, refusing to deal with anyone but the leader.

The rebel gestures toward the jeep with his AK47.

The leader jumps off a Jeep, and letting out a bark of laughter, he slowly walks toward me. "So this is the new head of the Hemsley family?" His tone is condescending. When he stops in front of me, he laughs again, "Or the guard dog?"

I don't let him bait me, but instead, pin him with a deadly glare. "Did you bring the diamonds?" I get right to the point.

He nods, his eyes sharpening on me as he waves a hand in the air. "Money?"

"Diamonds first," I growl.

Tension begins to run high as one of the rebels opens a tin containing the diamonds, and the rest of the rebels dismount the jeeps.

I hold up a hand, gesturing for Winter to come to me. The skin prickles on the back of my neck until she's next to me, with Cillian on her other side.

The leader's eyes rove over her, and then he smirks.

My heart falters as Winter moves forward. She lifts her chin, her eyes twin flames as she faces off with the rebels.

She holds her hand, palm up, and then Gbao nods.

The rebel drops a single diamond in her hand, and I watch the men closely while Winter performs the sandpaper test. Then she mutters, "I'll choose the next one." She takes another and checks it. "We're good."

My senses are on high alert, my skin prickling, and my breaths slow. "Bring the money."

Cillian walks back to the plane and seconds later returns with the briefcase. He sets it down on the ground, and opening it, he steps back to Winter's side.

Gbao eyes the money then makes a lazy gesture for one of his men to take it.

Silence fills the air as they hand the tin of diamonds to Winter, and neither group turn their back on the other as we slowly retreat to the plane.

Only when we're on the aircraft, and I shut the door behind us, do my muscles begin to relax. I remain standing by the door, my weapon ready as we taxi down the dusty runway.

Gunfire erupts, then Cillian says, "They're leaving. Just firing into the air. Nothing to worry about."

When we take off from Sierra Leone soil, I walk to Winter and take the seat next to her. I set the weapon down and suck in a deep breath of air.

"That went much better than I expected," Winter mutters as she inspects every diamond. "The way the two of you went on, I was expecting some fun."

Cillian lets out a chuckle. "Only you'd call it boring."

"Not every meeting will be that easy," I grumble. Still, I'm proud of how Winter held her own. She didn't bristle under pressure. Not that I expected her to.

"When will we do the drop?" she asks.

"Next month."

"Will Alexei meet us in New York?" She closes the tin and hands it to Cillian, who places it in a briefcase.

"Yes."

Winter's eyes settle on my face, and then she smiles at me. "We should celebrate our first successful run."

"A barbeque, a bonfire, and a pint of beer," Cillian mutters.

It makes Winter chuckle. "Just like father did every time he got home."

"Sounds good," I agree, just relieved nothing went wrong. God, I hope it will get easier with time having Winter along on the runs because I know for a fact my wife won't back down.

Chapter 27

WINTER

Seated around the bonfire pit, I have a soft smile on my face as I watch Cillian down another beer. "Nectar of the Gods," he muses as he sets his beer mug down.

Dana immediately fills it again, to which Cillian says, "Are you trying to get me drunk, woman?"

"Of course," she teases him.

"Oh." His eyebrows lift, then he gives her a lopsided grin. "Will you take advantage of me then?"

I let out a sputter of laughter. "Eww. I'm right here."

Looking awkward, Cillian mutters, "Sorry, poppet."

Damien sits down next to me and places his hand on my thigh, his grip tight. He just showered, and with his hair damp and his aftershave filling the air I breathe, I say, "I should get you drunk, so I can take advantage of you." My eyes drop to the black shirt that spans tightly over his chest, and then I drink in his muscular legs.

Cillian lets out a groan. "Payback's a bitch."

Damien turns his gaze to me, and seeing my desire for him on my face, his lips curve up. "You don't have to get me drunk."

"Christ have mercy," Cillian mumbles as he lifts the beer to his mouth.

I let out a burst of laughter which makes Damien smile.

"This is nice," I murmur.

Dana goes to get the steaks from the kitchen and puts Cillian to work so he'll grill them. Soon the aroma fills the air, and I let out a happy sigh.

Damien presses a kiss to my temple, and wrapping his arm around me, he pulls me into his side. "Are you happy?"

I nod, my cheek brushing against his shirt. "Very."

I watch as the flames dance, shooting embers into the night sky. Dana and Cillian's flirting and chuckles drift from where they're barbequing.

God, what more could I want from this life? I have Damien Vetrov as my husband. I have Dana and Cillian. The business will continue to thrive.

Life is perfect.

In the week following the run, we all find a routine. Damien and I plan the future runs and sales for the coming month, while Cillian keeps an eye on the guards and grounds.

"Congo's next?" I ask to make sure as I sift through my father's documents. I decided to clean out the office so Damien and I can make it our own. I'll pack away Dad and Sean's personal belongings at some point, but I'm not ready for that yet.

"Yes, next week. We're meeting on Thursday," Damien answers from where he's setting the code on the new vault he installed today.

"What's the code?" I glance up from the papers in my hand.

"Our wedding day. The year, then the month, and the date," he murmurs as he locks the code in. When he turns to me, I reward him with a smile.

I turn my attention back to the documents and let out a sigh. "Lord only knows why my father kept these. Receipts for coffee? Why?"

"Who knows," Damien murmurs as he takes a seat. I have everything on the encrypted laptop so just throw the documents away."

I shove it into a box. "You're right."

Damien begins to help, and then he freezes. He drops the papers he was holding and picks up a photo. His lips curve up into a smile I haven't seen before. "What are you looking at?"

He turns it so I can see. "Oh, I was ten." It's a photo of Mom, Sean, and me from when we still lived in Ireland.

Damien stares at the photo again. "Little Winter." He sets the photo aside, then asks, "Do you miss Ireland?"

"Sometimes," I answer as I load another stack of documents into the box. "And you? Do you miss Russia?"

Damien shakes his head. "It hasn't been home for a long time."

"Same," I agree. "This is home. The island." Damien only smiles, and it has me asking, "Does the island feel like home to you?"

His eyes lift to mine. "You're my home, Princess. I don't care where we live." He continues to sift through the documents, and then he opens a folder, and a frown forms on his face.

"What's that?" I ask as he slowly pages through whatever's in the folder.

I get up so I can see as he says, "Photos of us at the academy."

"What?" I move closer and then glance at the photos. There's one of us jogging around the academy. Another is of us during training. There's also one where Damien's gaze is locked on me while I'm having dinner with Adrien.

"God, there's so many," I gasp as I take a couple, looking through them. My father had me watched while I was at St. Monarch's. "Look." I hold a photo of Damien carrying me. It must've been after Vince drugged me. "This was two days before the auction. My father said nothing of him knowing about the attack."

Damien shows me one where I have my arm hooked through his, and we're staring at each other. "The first night before dinner."

I put down the photos and look at a printout of Damien's accomplishments. There's also correspondence between Madame Keller and my father where she tells him we have an unusual bond, and Dad makes his interest clear he wants to bid on Damien for me.

"The greatest gift he gave me," I murmur.

DAMIEN

Carson called after he successfully completed his contract. It feels as if we haven't seen each other in months, yet it's only been four weeks.

I stand by the piers as I watch a boat approach the island, and then a smile forms on my face when I see Carson. He brings the boat to a stop next to the dock and tosses me a rope. I tie it to a pole and then hold my hand out to him. He takes it with a wide grin, and as soon as he steps onto the dock, we embrace each other.

"You got married," Carson chuckles as he pulls back to grab his bag.

"Your brother's doing," I mutter. We stare at each other, then I ask, "You've been well?"

He nods as I gesture for him to walk. "The contract was successful. I had no problems."

"Good." I glance at him. "What's next? Will you join Alexei?"

To my surprise, Carson shakes his head. "Not yet. I like being a lone wolf." His gaze roams over the island, then he asks, "How's married life?"

"Good." Carson gives me a questioning look, and it has me elaborating, "It's very good." My words draw a chuckle from him.

As we near the house, Winter comes out the back door, and then I admit, "There's no getting her out of my system. I love her."

"I'm happy for you, brother," Carson says, his words genuine.

"You're not pissed off that I won't be joining you?" I ask, not wanting there to be any bad blood between us.

"No. I'll be fine on my own. Besides," he gestures at the grounds surrounding the house, "I like having a place I can escape to between contracts."

"You'll always be welcome," I say just before we reach Winter.

When Carson hugs her, Winter's eyes widen, and she stands frozen. He lets her go, then laughs, "You're family now."

Her lips curve up. "So you don't want to kill me for stealing your custodian."

Carson lets out another burst of laughter. "I lost him the moment he laid eyes on you. I didn't kill you then, so there's no reason to worry now."

"Carson Koslov," Cillian says from the backdoor. "While you're here, I want to hire you to take out Damien for marrying Winter behind my back."

Carson's eyes snap to me, and it has me chuckling. "He's joking."

"Don't make jokes like that," Winter chastises Cillian as she pushes him back into the house.

"Seems you got a father-in-law anyway," Carson mutters.

"At least once a day, he wants to kick my ass," I chuckle. Meeting Carson's gaze, I explain, "It's our way of bonding."

"Come. Show me your house," Carson says, throwing an arm around my shoulder.

Walking inside, I introduce Carson to Dana before I take him to the living room. Carson sets his bag down while I pour us each a shot of Vodka.

"Na zdoróv'je," we toast before swallowing the shot down.

Carson glances around then his eyes meet mine again. "How's the diamond business?"

We take a seat as I answer, "Good. We had a successful run, and the next one is on Thursday. I was hoping you'd come with."

"Of course. I'd like to see what you do now," he agrees.

"Are you sure you can only stay the week?" I ask.

"Yes, I want to visit Alexei before my next contract."

I nod as Winter comes into the living room. She takes a seat next to me, then smiles at Carson. "Do you know who your next contract is?"

Carson shakes his head. "Not yet."

We visit until it's time for dinner, and then we move to the dining room.

When Dana places a feast on the table, Carson says, "God, it looks good. I've been living off junk." Then he grins at me. "No wonder you're picking up weight."

My eyebrows dart up as Cillian chuckles, and then I mutter, "I'll kick both your asses in the barn tomorrow."

"Oh, it's on," Cillian says, a grin spreading over his face.

Winter takes her seat on my right, and I reach for her hand, giving it a squeeze before we help ourselves to the delicious food.

While eating, banter and laughter fill the air, and as I glance around the table, I take in my family with a smile curving my lips.

I never knew something like this existed, not until Winter. My gaze drifts to her, and I'm met with her warm smile.

To think, I get to wake up to her beautiful face every morning. I get to watch men submit to her while she bends the knee to only me.

"I love you," I murmur softly, now understanding the true meaning of the emotion.

Epilogue

DAMIEN

Fifteen years later...

Crouching next to Inna, our seven-year-old little girl, I murmur, "Take a deep breath, then you slowly let it out before pulling the trigger."

Inna nods then lines the barrel up with her sight. I watch as she inhales and exhales, and then her tiny finger pulls the trigger.

When the paintball splats over Cillian's back and he lets out a curse, I grab hold of Inna and make a run for cover.

"Little shits," Cillian shouts after us.

Inna's laughter explodes through the forest, and it has me covering her mouth as I try not to laugh myself. "Shh, we need to be silent."

"Silent my butt," Nikolai, our eleven-year-old son, chuckles, and then a paintball hits my leg. "Mom, I got Dad," he yells.

I don't stop running and pointing my gun at Nikolai, I shoot him in the stomach, bright yellow splatting over his black shirt. "Dad!" he shouts, and then he runs after me just as Winter breaks through the trees.

Inna clings to me like a monkey, ducking her head against my neck as paintballs splat against my back. Dramatically, I drop to my knees, groaning, "Save yourself, Inna. Run."

"Don't be silly, Daddy," she sasses me, and then she opens fire on her mother and brother. No one has the heart to shoot her, and I crawl behind my daughter for cover.

"Grown ass man hiding behind a kid," Cillian mutters as he tries to get past Inna. Suddenly Cillian darts forward, and he grabs hold of Inna, throwing her over his shoulder, and it has her screeching, "That's cheating, Grandpa."

She aims the gun at his ass and pulls the trigger, and then I'm struggling to breathe as laughter explodes from me.

Cillian puts her down and drops to his knees while grabbing hold of his ass. Inna gives him a self-accomplished look. "I'm the Blood Princess. No one messes with me."

Nikolai shoots me one more time, and then I dart up, and his shrill scream echoes through the forest as I chase after him. He got his mother's speed.

"Mom!" Nikolai shouts as he darts through the trees. "Help!"

A paintball splats against my back, and then another. I come to a stop and turn to Winter, who's grinning at me. I dart forward and quickly grab hold her, yanking her against my body, and then I smear the paint on my neck all over her face.

She lets out a screech of laughter and seeing how happy she is, I claim her lips.

"Eww," Inna suddenly says, making Winter chuckle again.

"If it weren't for eww, you wouldn't –"

"Cillian!" Winter hushes him before he can complete the sentence. "She's only seven."

"I wouldn't what?" Inna asks as Nikolai walks back to us.

"Your Mom will smack me. Let's go wash off the paint," Cillian says as he takes hold of Inna's hand.

We walk back to the house, the atmosphere playful, until Dana spots us. "You're not stepping a foot inside this house looking like that."

"Aww, come on, love," Cillian chuckles as he starts to run for her. Dana lets out a shriek and disappears inside.

"Everyone, shower before dinner," Winter says as we walk inside.

We scatter to our rooms, and I make sure to lock the door before I follow Winter to the shower.

Winter opens the faucets, and then we undress, my eyes still drinking in the sight of her naked body.

"Come here," I growl as I pull her under the spray.

"Did you lock the door?" she asks as she wraps her arms around my neck.

"Yes." I lower my head and claim my wife's mouth.

It's been fifteen years, and I still haven't had my fill of her. Another hundred years wouldn't be enough, not with Winter and her fiery spirit keeping the fire burning in my heart.

The End.

Published Books

STANDALONE NOVELS
Mafia / Organized Crime / Suspense Romance

MERCILESS SAINTS
Damien Vetrov

CRUEL SAINTS
Lucian Cotroni

RUTHLESS SAINTS
Carson Koslov

TEARS OF BETRAYAL
Demitri Vetrov

TEARS OF SALVATION
Alexei Koslov
A Standalone for The Underworld Kings Collaboration.

Enemies To Lovers

College Romance / New Adult / Billionaire Romance

Heartless
Reckless
Careless
Ruthless
Shameless
False Perceptions

Trinity Academy

College Romance / New Adult / Billionaire Romance

Falcon
Mason
Lake
Julian
The Epilogue

The Heirs

College Romance / New Adult / Billionaire Romance

Coldhearted Heir
Arrogant Heir

Defiant Heir
Loyal Heir
Callous Heir
Sinful Heir
Tempted Heir
Forbidden Heir

Not My Hero
Young Adult / High School Romance

The Southern Heroes Series

*Suspense Romance / Contemporary Romance /
Police Officers & Detectives*

The Ocean Between Us
The Girl In The Closet
The Lies We Tell Ourselves
All The Wasted Time
We Were Lost

Connect with me

Newsletter

FaceBook

Amazon

GoodReads

BookBub

Instagram

About the author

Michelle Heard is a Wall Street Journal, and USA Today Bestselling Author who loves creating stories her readers can get lost in. She resides in South Africa with her son where she's always planning her next book to write, and trip to take.

Want to be up to date with what's happening in Michelle's world? Sign up to receive the latest news on her alpha hero releases → NEWSLETTER

If you enjoyed this book or any book, please consider leaving a review. It's appreciated by authors.

Acknowledgments

Clarissa, thank you for your endless patience with me and for helping me. I hope I can repay the favor one day.

To my alpha and beta readers – Leeann, Sheena, Sherrie, Kelly, Allyson & Sarah, thank you for being the godparents of my paper-baby.

Candi Kane PR - Thank you for being patient with me and my bad habit of missing deadlines.

Yoly, Cormar Covers – Thank you for giving my paper-babies the perfect look.

To my readers, thank you for loving these characters as much as I do.

My street team, thank you for promoting my books. It means the world to me!

A special thank you to every blogger and reader who took the time to take part in the cover reveal and release day.

Love ya all tons ;)

Printed in Great Britain
by Amazon